OUR HONORED D.

A bullet races toward Detective Stephanie Chalice, a bullet meant to kill not one, but two. Chalice is pushed to her physical and mental limits as she investigates four murders, each with its own unique criminal signature. The murder trail takes her from Ground Zero in lower Manhattan to the icy narrows beneath the Verrazano Bridge as she pursues a villain, who is both clever and diabolical. A solitary strand of evidence ties the four murders together but is it enough for our hero to go on? Lives hang in the balance as the clock clicks down toward zero. Is Chalice's time about to run out?

~~~

The Stephanie Chalice Mystery Series

Don't Close Your Eyes

Ransom Beach

The Brain Vault

Our Honored Dead
~~~

Praise For Lawrence Kelter and The Stephanie Chalice Mystery Series

"Lawrence Kelter is an exciting new novelist, who reminds me of an early Robert Ludlum." **—Nelson DeMille**

"Chalice's acerbic repartee is like an arsenal of nuclear missiles." **—BookWire Review**

"Kelter is a master, pure and simple." **—Rachel Dove for Kindle Book Review**

"Chalice is irresistible; a contemporary tour de force." **—James Siegel, NY Times best-selling author of Derailed**

"Red-hot reading, hypnotic, atmospheric . . . Lawrence Kelter has a rare gift for intricate plotting, swift pacing, and well-drawn characters that jump off the page. A helluva psychological thriller." **—J.R. Rain, USA Today best-selling author of Moon Dance and Dark Horse**

"Lawrence Kelter is my kind of writer: blistering action, unforgettable characters, and dialogue sharp enough to draw blood. Kelter gives more bang for the buck than any thriller writer I know." **—Dani Amore, best-selling author of Dead Wood**

"Lawrence Kelter just keeps getting better and better. Fast pace, action, and humor; what more can you ask for in a great read? This one's a must!" **—Rick Murcer, NY Times best-selling author of Caribbean Moon**

Our Honored Dead

By

Lawrence Kelter

First Edition – November 2012

ISBN-13: 978-1480130852 ISBN-10: 1480130852

Edited by
Jan Green of thewordverve inc

Interior book design by
Bob Houston eBook Formatting

For Dawn and Chris

Acknowledgments

The author gratefully acknowledges the following special people for their contributions to this book.

For my wife, Isabella, for her love, support, and tireless dedication to the perfection of this book.

For my children, Dawn and Chris for making me smile.

Our Honored Dead

Stephanie Chalice Mystery #4

By
Lawrence Kelter

“And if any mischief follow, then thou shalt give life for life . . .”

~Exodus 21:23-25~

Prologue

As I looked out the hospital window at the sobering morning sky, I wondered why God would allow this to happen. I was losing all of the great men in my life, one by one: first my dad and now Sonellio. He had always meant so much to me. He was like the uncle I never had, one of my father's contemporaries, and a guiding force in my life.

I swallowed, hoping the pop in my ears would block out the monotonous beep of the heart monitor. It was early in the morning, so damn early, not quite six. *Too early to lose him*, I told myself. *Please give us the day, just one more day. I'm not ready.* I turned from the window to drink him in, perhaps for the last time, and hope for a miracle. His face was pale. Each breath was so tentative that I was uncertain another would follow.

I folded my arms over my belly as if to protect the new life within from the influence of death. "He's a good man," I whispered, "a really good man." A few tears began to drizzle down my cheek.

The baby kicked.

"Don't be upset, there's nothing we can do."

The baby kicked again as if to challenge me.

"Settle down." I rubbed my belly in a soothing manner. "You're just like your father, always looking for attention."

God takes with one hand and gives back with the other, one life ebbing away and a new one about to arrive. Anyone in my position would have entertained the same thought.

"What's that you say, I'm being morose? You know you're very precocious for a fetus."

The baby kicked twice in rapid succession.

"Anyway, I'm sorry if I'm sad. I can't help it. I love him a lot."

I heard the floor creak. I was still a little on edge from the events that had just transpired. To say there were loose ends in our investigation was an understatement. A murderer was still at large. I usually have my emotions under control, but with all of my hormones whirling around like spirits in a cocktail shaker . . . I turned and looked through the doorway into the hospital corridor. All was quiet.

Sonellio moaned. His desperate sound drew my attention. I stroked his cheek. "Nothing to worry about, Boss, everything will be all right."

Thinking back, Sonellio had always been around. My father had worked for him when he was on the job. He had always been there for me after dad passed.

"Hey, stop kicking," I scolded the baby playfully. "I'm going to miss him. I'm sorry." He became my boss after I made the cut and became a detective. He was a good, salt-of-the-earth, church-going, Italian boy with great morals. But Sonellio had smoked heavily. It was a solitary chink in the armor of a noble man, a weakness that was about to put him into the ground. Lung cancer. It could have all been prevented. It was difficult to remember him as the healthy, younger man I had once known. *To see him now, so gaunt; you would never believe it was the same person.*

"You're never going to smoke," I informed the baby.

I felt the baby move.

"It's not negotiable."

My stomach rumbled. This time it was due to

hunger. "I hope daddy gets here with mommy's coffee soon. It's okay, Sweetie; it's only decaf. Yes, that's right. I've given up regular coffee, just for you."

The baby was still trying to get comfortable.

"Anything for you, Sweetie."

The baby grew fidgety.

"Yes, even the red wine; that's gone too. No, I don't mind."

Sonellio moaned again, more deeply than before. I wondered if he was out of time. He had been moaning since I arrived, a low and even sound that accompanied his shallow breathing. He moaned again, louder still. There was something unnerving about the sound of it. It sounded as if he was agitated. It was almost as if he sensed something and was trying to give me a warning.

The baby abruptly stopped fidgeting and became calm.

I felt goose bumps rise on my arms and neck.

"Chalice!"

My heart skipped a beat. I was waiting for Gus to return and was expecting to hear the loving tone of his voice.

The voice I heard was not his.

There was something disturbing and strange in the sound of the voice I had just heard. My heart became still.

It seemed like moments passed.

My heart finally began to beat again.

I turned.

My eyes locked on the gun that was pointed at my baby and me. I instinctively covered my belly with my hands to protect my baby as any mother would, but we were out in the open, naked and vulnerable. I cried out in terror, *"Gus!"*

And then I heard the sound of the gun fire.

Chapter One

Weeks earlier.

The sign on the door read, Phillip Kranston, OBGYN. I had been seeing Dr. Kranston for years, for his expertise as a GYN and was now getting to know him as an OB. He looked like Charles Nelson Reilly and wore glasses with massive frames. He is the sweetest man, completely innocent and unassuming. He would sometimes call at 10:00 at night or later to discuss lab results. I didn't know of too many doctors as dedicated as he was. Phillip Kranston definitely fell within a small circle of individuals I trusted unconditionally. I referred all of my friends to him. *I mean look, I trust him to examine my hoo-ha. How many men can you say that about?*

His waiting room was painted a warm shade of plum. The furniture was clear oak.

I was feeling a wee bit green.

I sat down with a clipboard—attached was a registration form and a medical survey with more questions than you might expect to find on the New York State Bar Exam. Kranston's office was very efficient, and they asked for a profile update on every visit. Nothing had changed since the last visit, so I ran through the forms, checking boxes without giving it too much thought.

A woman sat next to me nursing her little girl. Her infant seemed content with her lunch, suckling happily on mommy's breast. She turned to me, and we exchanged a brief smile just as the waiting room door burst open and another pregnant woman in leggings and pencil heels rushed into the room. She raced up to the reception window.

"Cassandra Capuano for Dr. Kranston," she said, panting.

The receptionist checked her schedule. "You're an hour late."

"Yeah, yeah, I'm sorry," Cassandra said, "The cab driver got lost."

The receptionist answered with a pleasant smile. "I know; this place is a little hard to find."

"Hard to find?" Cassandra said. "The cab driver drove past it four times. Honey, this place is a friggin' mirage. I think Bin Laden hid here."

The receptionist's eyes grew wide. "Please have a seat," she said. "I'll get you in as soon as I can."

"Thanks, sweetie, I've got a mani and pedi in forty-five minutes; see what you can do."

Cassandra waddled away and sat down next to me. "Waiting long, honey?" she asked.

"Just sat down," I replied.

Cassandra opened her purse, took out her compact, and blotted her nose. "Jesus Christ, these *f-ing* hormones. I'm sweating like a pig. Do you sweat a lot?"

"Sometimes. Not now, thank God."

Cassandra glanced up at me. "You're hardly showing."

"It's pretty early on."

"You're a big girl. You're going to need custom made bras before this is over."

I shrugged. I mean we were hardly BFFs, and I wasn't sure Cassandra was the kind of girl I wanted to bond with.

"It's okay, don't be modest. Honey, I'd kill for boobs

like that. Me—" She lifted her butt out of the chair and patted her rump. "I've got it all in the ass. My husband loves it, thank God." Cassandra laughed. It sounded like someone was strangling a chicken. "I can't pry him off with a crowbar."

O-M-G, T-M-I.

"My husband's a DJ. He spins at all of the hottest clubs in the city. Maybe you've heard of him—he calls himself DJ Sammy Stash," she said proudly.

Once again, O-M-G. When did DJ become an official title? No disrespect to the profession, and maybe I'm a little old-fashioned, but since when did the designation DJ rise to the level of the more commonly heralded titles like: Doctor, Father, and Officer? "Sorry, no, I haven't had the pleasure." DJ Sammy Stash for God's sake—was he a disc jockey or a drug dealer? I guarantee this guy had a rap sheet.

The baby being nursed let out a loud burp. Her mother smiled. "You're such a little piggy," she said playfully. She tickled her little girl, eliciting a contented *coo*. She put her daughter on her shoulder and began to rub her back. "She's got *such* an appetite."

"God bless her, she's a big girl," Cassandra commented as she continued to check her face. "Maybe your diet is too rich. Do you eat a lot of fatty foods?"

From the look of disbelief on her face, I understood that the nursing mom was uncomfortable. I think she was torn about her choice of responses, perhaps straddling the fence between a polite "what do you mean?" and "fuck off!"

I smiled at the nursing mom to draw her attention and spare her the task of having to respond to Cassandra. "She's adorable. How old is she?" I asked.

"Eleven months." Her eyes said, *Thank you.*

"She's such a big, beautiful girl."

"Eighty-fifth percentile for height and weight," she said proudly. "Her father's tall." She took her baby off her shoulder and wiped her mouth. "You're a big girl, aren't you, aren't you, a big, beautiful girl?" Her baby smiled and clicked her tongue. "Your first?" she asked.

I nodded. "Yup, number one."

"You must be so excited," she said, happy to convey the blessing of expectant motherhood.

The receptionist opened her window. "Sophia Farrell."

"That's me," the nursing mom said. She fixed her blouse and gathered up a huge shoulder bag, which was filled to the brim with baby fixings. "Come on, sweetie," she said to her little girl. "It's mommy's turn. Nice chatting with you," she said to me. She glared at Cassandra as she stood, but the gesture went unnoticed.

"Same here." I waved to her baby. "Nice to meet you." Sophia walked through the inner doorway to the examination rooms.

"*You're* nice," Cassandra said to me as she closed her compact.

"What do you mean?"

"You said her baby was adorable."

"She is adorable. She's got such big cheeks."

"For real? Did you get a good look at the kisser on that baby?"

"Yes!"

"You really think that kid's adorable?"

"Yes," I said in an incredulous tone.

"Honey, that kid's a Cabbage Patch doll. Are you kidding me or what? It's a good thing that kid's too young to tell time because that face could stop a clock."

I glared at her. "That's really rude."

"Yeah, yeah, look, I know what you're going to say:

'all babies are beautiful.' Eleven months old, and she's ready to pop out another one. Christ, the city ought to declare an ordinance on having too many homely kids."

"Stephanie Chalice." The receptionist was standing by the open door waiting for me. *Oh, thank God.* I got up immediately. I should've put Cassandra in her place, but I didn't. I walked away without responding to her. There are some people that just aren't worth the effort. *I hope she catches a toe fungus at the nail salon.* I couldn't imagine how *her* child was going to turn out.

The entrance door opened, and Gus Lido bolted through. He caught up with me.

"You're just in time, daddy."

Gus smiled at his newly earned title. "I couldn't find a parking spot; finally threw it into a parking lot."

"No problem—they just called me in."

We followed the doctor's assistant to the examination room. She took my vitals and handed me a gown. "Dr. Kranston will be in to see you in just a few minutes." She stepped out and closed the door.

"Want to help me change?" I asked Gus. I unfolded the boxy gown and held it up for him to see. "Pretty sexy, huh?"

Gus put his arms around me and gave me a kiss. "You look incredible. There's something about you that's just driving me crazy."

"Ma says that I've got *the glow.*"

He pressed his forehead to mine. "How much longer did you say it was okay for us to do it?"

"Do it?"

Gus smiled knowingly. "Yeah, do it."

"Don't fret, Romeo. We're good in the sack until at least the seventh month. I'll let you know when you need to begin the cold shower routine."

"Are you sure? Maybe you want to check with the

doctor."

"*No.* I don't have to ask the doctor. I know what I'm talking about. There's a lot of material on the subject. Maybe you should read a book about it too." Gus had some misplaced concern that his doodad might accidently damage the baby. *I mean Gus is a real man, but let's not get ridiculous.*

"No, that's okay. I'll trust you on it." He kissed me on the nape of the neck.

I pushed him away. "*No, absolutely not.* There's a commandment about not getting busy in the baby doctor's office." I pulled my blouse off over my head.

"Oh dear God," he whined. "Look at you—how many more months?"

"You sound like you're going through withdrawal. What's up? I haven't kicked you out of the bed yet."

I kicked off my shoes and had begun to take off my slacks before I remembered there would be no stirrups today. *Thank God.* We were only there for a follow-up sonogram.

I zipped my slacks back up. Gus whined again.

Down boy. I stuck my butt out and smacked it. "Does our baby make my ass look fat?" Gus looked perplexed—his expression slowly changed into a smile.

I quickly slipped into the examination gown.

Dr. Kranston knocked on the door. "Are you ready?" He had been practicing for decades and yet still seemed embarrassed when he entered the examination room.

"Ready," I replied.

Dr. Kranston entered, sporting a big smile. "Hi, Stephanie." I gave him a kiss on the cheek." He blushed before he turned toward Gus. "Great to see you again, Gus."

Kranston gestured to the examination table. "Assume the position," he said with a silly chuckle.

I slid onto the table while Kranston entered data into the computer. “Do you say that to all of your patients or just the lady cops?”

“You’re so silly, Stephanie,” he snickered. He approached me with a bottle of ultrasound-sound gel and the transducer thingamabob. “Such a joyful occasion; I love delivering babies for two people who are so in love,” Kranston said. “Are we hoping for a boy or a girl?”

“I’ll take whatever the good Lord is handing out.” The truth was that all I wanted was a happy and healthy baby. The rest didn’t matter.

Kranston squeezed the lube on my belly. He began to move the ultra-sound doohickey around, and then of all the comments that could have possibly come out of his mouth: “It’s okay for the two of you to enjoy each other during the pregnancy.”

My mouth dropped. “Excuse me?”

“It’s okay for the two of you to continue having sex,” Kranston said. “There are lots of preconceived notions about harming the baby, but none of it is true.” He was focused on the monitor as he spoke. He was in his own world and completely oblivious to the fact that he was torturing me with embarrassment. “Although,” he continued, “anal sex is not a good idea.”

Jesus, Mary, and Joseph, did he just say “anal sex?” I was mortified. I looked at Kranston; he was clueless. He had no idea I was dying a thousand deaths.

“For how long?” Gus asked eagerly.

My God, does it get any worse? I can’t believe this conversation. It was a good thing Gus was so hot because I was seriously considering shutting my doors for the duration.

I glared at Gus. *Could this conversation possibly be any more inappropriate?* “What makes you so sure I’ll even want to?"

"But, but . . ." Gus actually began to stammer.

Kranston finally looked up from the sonogram monitor. "Yup," he said, "Everything looks good."

Chapter Two

Anya Kozakova sat at her kitchen table staring at the envelope that had been delivered by messenger almost an hour earlier. She glanced up at the wall clock: 3:50 p.m.; she had ten minutes to make up her mind.

In or out? She drummed her fingers on the tabletop while she pondered her decision. She was stuck. She glanced at the clock again: 3:55 p.m. "In or out?" she grumbled, "In or out?" She had performed services like this before—illegal services. The money was good, but the anxiety was terrible, and she worried about getting caught and deported. She had worked steadily since coming to the United States but always as a consultant and never as an employee. She worked off the books to avoid paying taxes.

She heard her neighbors moaning through the paper-thin walls of her Brooklyn apartment. They were always home, either drunk or going at it—this time both. "Shut up!" she yelled in a voice loud enough to be heard through the wall. She hated having to shout, but her neighbors were inconsiderate. Their selfish and incessant cavorting made it easy for her to absolve herself of any guilt.

"I've got to get out of this rat hole." In the next instant, she grabbed the envelope, tore it open, and turned it upside down. A cell phone tumbled out. It was a throw-away phone, a phone with no contract, which had been preloaded with minutes. It was a phone that could not be traced—or so she had been told. She switched it on and waited for it to boot.

A solitary phone number was already saved as a Favorite. She looked up at the clock; it was 4:00 p.m., and the second hand had just swept past numeral twelve. She pressed her finger on the highlighted number—the call connected.

"Do you have something to tell me?"

She hesitated a moment and then realized her throat was too dry to speak. She took a quick sip of water. "I'll do it."

Chapter Three

No one likes paperwork, especially me. Lieutenant Pamela Shearson was my new boss. She had been treating me differently ever since Gus and I officially declared our relationship and my pregnancy. She assigned me fewer cases, which meant that I had to spend more workdays in the squad room and fewer days out in the field. I was not good at the administrative part of the job. I found it tedious and boring. I preferred to work outdoors and get my hands dirty. For me, dirty hands equaled happy girl.

Shearson was a tough one. She had high aspirations and was not the type to let anyone get in her way, least of all me. I believed Shearson saw me as a threat, because I was younger and better liked. I might have been the happiest pregnant woman of all times, and I wouldn't have done anything differently, but by becoming pregnant, I had played right into her hands. So there I was in the squad room, doing paperwork, away from the action, just where Shearson wanted me.

I saw Gus running around the office. It gave me a chance to study him in a new light. I watched the way he walked and went about his activities. I thought about our baby as an adult and wondered if he or she would move around as Gus does. Gus walked in long strides, catlike, almost like a panther. He was powerful and purposeful. If those traits found their way to our child, well then, we had better have a boy. A girl who walked like that would look absolutely goofy.

"Chalice." Oh my God, Shearson's voice cut through me like a knife. She had a shrill voice that bypassed the ears and hit the nervous system directly.

"Yes, Lieutenant?"

Shearson was at my desk before I could stand up. She wore a Dries Van Noten dress which I recognized from an issue of Vogue. You could say anything you wanted about her, but you couldn't criticize her fashion sense. She made clothing look good. Shearson was married to an investment banker. She worked NYPD for the power and not for the bucks. "So what's the deal, Chalice, no baby bump yet?"

I put my hand on my stomach. "A little one."

"I hope that I'll look like you if I get pregnant. You've got some good genes."

I couldn't wait to share what she said with Gus. He would no doubt have a comment akin to: *I thought coldblooded creatures were egg layers.* "Your dress is gorgeous."

"I have to wear couture to get noticed. You look good in anything."

"Thanks, Lieutenant."

"Look, Chalice, you know that I've had you in slow mode. I figure why have you running around taking chances when you don't need to. I mean why put the little one in harm's way, correct?"

"Thanks, I appreciate your concern." *Yeah right. If only that was her primary motive.*

"Are you up to a little field work?"

Am I? "Most definitely, Lieutenant. The squad room bores me to tears."

"I thought so. Round up Lido and come into my office."

"What do you have?"

"I just received a special request from the FBI. Your

friend Ambler likes you a lot. Do you have incriminating photos of him stashed away or something?" she said with a smile. "I never saw a Fed that liked a city cop the way Ambler likes you."

"He and my dad go way back. Ambler's extended family."

"I thought I had heard that. Grab Lido and hurry back. You're needed downtown, chop-chop."

Shearson turned around so fast that she didn't see the huge smile on my face. I jumped out of my chair to track down Gus. I caught up with him as he was coming out of the men's room. "We've been sprung!"

"The Lieutenant has a case for us?"

I nodded like an excited schoolgirl.

"Oh thank God. I couldn't take another night of your complaining about how bored you are in the squad room."

"You know I'm not a desk jockey. Ambler requested our help on an FBI investigation."

"I love Ambler," Gus said. "Maybe I should treat him to a massage or something."

I wound a ringlet of hair around my finger and gave him a look that said, *wanna play?* "Well, if you really need a happy ending . . ."

"I thought Shearson was waiting for us?"

"Oh yeah, that's right." I grabbed his hand and we dashed off.

Chapter Four

“**Yee-haw**!”

Gus glanced over at me from the driver’s seat. “Excited, are we?”

“You bet! I’m going to give Ambler a big fat juicy kiss the minute I lay eyes on him. It must have killed Shearson to give us this assignment. She kept going on and on about not wanting to put me in harm’s way because I was pregnant, but I know better. She’s the most insincere woman I’ve ever met in my life.”

“I think it’s safe to say that you don’t like her. I mean you’re not going to invite her over for a pajama party or something like that, are you?”

“No, no pajama parties. Although I’d give a week’s pay to see what a woman like that wears to bed. I’ll bet she’s into whips and chains.” Gus rolled his eyes and then turned his attention back to the downtown traffic. We were on our way to Battery Park for a rendezvous with Herbert Ambler. “Hard for anyone to say ‘no’ to Ambler these days. My friend is finally getting some well-deserved recognition.”

“You think he’ll get that promotion?”

“God, I hope so. He’s so dedicated. I can’t think of anyone more deserving.”

“Special Agent in Charge, New York Field Office, Criminal Division is a big promotion. We should throw him a party.”

“I thought you were going to take him to a massage parlor.”

"I said that I was going to take him for a massage. I didn't say I was taking him for a *rub and tug*. I resent the implication," Gus said, pretending to be offended.

"*Please.* I know how the male mind works—you pick out a pretty eighteen-year old K-girl and then it's: *massage my neck, rub my shoulders . . . stroke my johnson—you've got lotion on your hands, why let it go to waste?*"

"K-girl? Did you just say K-girl?"

"Yeah, K-girl, as in a Korean hooker. Don't pretend that you don't know what it means."

"You're cynical." Gus leaned over and patted me on the leg. "Don't worry, baby; you're the only one stroking *my* johnson."

I pretended to wipe a tear from my eye. "That's what I love about you, baby; you're so romantic." Gus gave me a silly smile. "Okay, we'll throw him a party. He deserves it."

"No K-girls?"

I gave Gus a harsh sneer.

We pulled up at the intersection of Liberty and West. I could see a crime scene team at work no more than a hundred feet away. My dear friend Herbert Ambler was standing curbside as we pulled up. He opened the door for me. I got out of the car and gave him a huge hug. "Well, good morning, Mr. Special Officer Herbert Ambler." I adore the man. I gave him a kiss on the cheek. He may have moved up in the world, but his appearance had not changed. He looked the same way he always did with the barbershop crew cut and the aviator glasses. "Are you all set with that?"

"Yes, thanks to you."

"Thanks to me? What the hell are you talking about?"

"You found the Chinese ambassador's son. It was a

toss-up between Rodriguez and me as to who was going to get the job. Finding R.C. Liu's son sealed the deal."

"Oh, stop the self-deprecating crap. You got the job because you deserve it."

"Yes, that and because I associate with the right people. Liu's son was about to be decapitated. You're the one that found him in the underground tunnel beneath Pilgrim State Mental Hospital. You made me look like a hero. I've wanted this promotion for a long time. Frank and Lisa Chalice raised one hell of a smart cop."

"Stop it. You're going to make me cry."

Gus caught up with us just in the nick of time. The two men bro-hugged. "Are congratulations in order?" Gus asked.

"It's official," I boasted on Ambler's behalf.

Gus hugged him again. He could get emotional at times. The three of us had been through a lot together.

"Stop it," Ambler said. "You'll have me singing 'Kumbaya' in two minutes." He pulled away from Gus.

"So what's going on over there?" I said as I looked over Ambler's shoulder at the crime scene activity.

"Ready to get busy, Chalice?" Ambler said. "Let's see if you can make me look good one more time."

Chapter Five

"**Now** there's something you don't see every day." Kowsky Plaza is a recreational area not far from Battery Park, replete with a promenade and a dog run. The key focal point, however, is a twelve-foot-tall section of the original Berlin Wall. It's painted with a primitive drawing of a bright-green, elongated face with red, bulbous lips. A wrought-iron fence encloses the two and three-quarter ton section of concrete. It didn't, however, stop someone from depositing a body at the base of the wall. The process of collecting and cataloging evidence was in full swing as we approached. "Are we here to investigate a murder or locate the perpetrator of that horrific piece of art?"

"I see pregnancy hasn't taken the edge off your incredibly sarcastic sense of humor," Ambler said.

"Some things never change," Gus said with a chuckle.

"It was a gift from the German Consulate and came from downtown Berlin," Ambler said. "It prevented East Germans from escaping."

"Because the wall was so high?" Gus asked.

"No, because the East Germans took one look at that big, green face and tossed their cookies. Speaking of which, I forgot to bring my barf bag."

Ambler rolled his eyes. "Are you going to be okay—I mean being pregnant and all?"

"Chalice women are tough. I'll deal. So what's going on here?"

"The body was discovered around dawn," Ambler said. "This is not the scene of the murder. The body was deposited here postmortem."

"No blood?" Gus asked.

"No blood, no identification, no witnesses, and no—"

"Let me guess, no clues?"

"Oh there's a clue all right, a strange one. That's one of the reasons why I asked for your help."

"I thought you wanted my recipe for chicken cacciatore."

Ambler smirked. "All right, let's take a closer look," he said. "Time to get busy."

Cinder blocks had been stacked on both sides of the wrought-iron fence—jury-rigged stairs, if you will. They provided enough additional height for us to step over the pickets without spearing our respective man and lady parts. The victim was a young Caucasian male. He was dressed in a tight-fitting blazer and jeans, which were sopping wet. His hair was gelled and spiked. His complexion was gray. "Have we established the time of death?"

"He's in full rigor. I'd say he's been dead at least one day," Ambler said.

"He hasn't bloated yet," Gus said, "so he was kept cold—the inner cavity hasn't filled with gas yet."

"Any idea why he's so wet? It hasn't rained all week." I scanned the area. "I don't see any sprinkler heads."

"I could answer both questions, but I'd rather watch the two of you at work," Ambler said. "Put your gloves on and have at it."

Gus and I snapped on the latex and got busy examining John Doe. I knelt next to him and immediately felt waves of cold radiating from his body. I put my hand on his chest. "Jesus, he's frozen."

"You're a quick study," Ambler said. "That's why he's

wet, he's thawing."

"Yeah, like a big turkey in trendy clothes. I don't see any wounds. Is it possible he died of hypothermia?"

"Very possible," Ambler said. "We'll just have to wait for a coroner's report."

I examined the victim's face, head, and scalp. "No bruising anywhere." I looked up at Ambler. "So what's so special about a frozen man that the FBI has to call in NYPD for an assist?"

"You'll like this," Ambler said, "Check his teeth."

The crime scene investigators had left Doe's mouth partially open. I looked in and winced. The upper and lower incisors had been removed and not by a dental professional. The victim's mouth had been butchered. I started to feel nauseous. "You could have warned me, Herb. I am pregnant, you know."

Ambler chuckled. "Don't *wus* out on me, Chalice."

I stood up and took a deep breath and another and another. The nausea subsided. "I know you're setting me up. So where are his teeth?"

Ambler smiled and then waved to one of the crime scene investigators. The investigator handed Ambler an evidence bag. Ambler held up what looked like a small, tablet-shaped medallion, rectangular in shape and rounded on one end. It was attached to a leather thong. "This was around his neck," Ambler said. He turned the medallion so that we could get a better look. The front of the medallion was a blue ceramic mosaic. Teeth had been used to form the numeral two.

"That's different," Gus said.

"I'd say so." I turned to Ambler and asked the question that was ready to spring from the tip of my tongue. "Where is number one?"

Chapter Six

"**Oh**, we've got number one," Ambler said. "What's left of him anyway."

"Spill it!"

"Sure," Ambler replied. "Give me a lift back to Federal Plaza. I'll fill you in back at the office."

"You walked?" Gus asked.

"Yeah, I hoofed it." Ambler patted his belly. He always had a small paunch—it didn't appear to be any larger. "Haven't seen the inside of a gym in years—have to do something to keep fit. It was a short walk anyway."

We marched over to the car. Ambler seemed to have a little extra pep in his step. He opened the rear door and got in.

"You look happy, my friend. The new promotion seems to be agreeing with you," I said.

Gus got in and cranked the engine. He pulled away lickety-split.

"It's nice to be recognized," Ambler said. "I've been with the Bureau a long time, and I've been passed over before. After a while you start to think it's just never going to happen. You know what I mean?"

"I had no doubt that you were going to get it. I could feel it in my bones."

"You should have shared your feelings with me," Ambler chuckled. "I was as nervous as a hen."

I reached back over the seat and patted him on the leg. "I'm so proud of you." I tried not to show him that I was getting choked up. He was family to me. Ambler blushed, and I faced front before he could see that a tear had popped out.

We made it back to Federal Plaza in no time flat. Ambler walked through FBI headquarters looking purposeful and self-assured. It was easy to see how proud he was to have earned the new rank. He showed us directly to his new office.

"Wow! This is nice." Ambler's office was large and impressive. It was glass on the street and interior sides so that he had a view of the inner office as well as lower Manhattan. His furniture looked and smelled brand new—I recognized the unmistakable odor of petrochemicals. I ran my fingers along the back of the sofa. "Nothing like the bouquet of fresh Naugahyde."

"I love this office," Ambler said. He closed the door and walked over to the window. "I spent the last ten years sitting in a cubicle."

"You deserve it," Gus said as he joined Ambler at the window. "Did they give you a hot young secretary to go with the promotion?"

Ambler laughed. "I have to hire my own secretary. The old one retired with her boss."

"I'm perfectly willing to help you out in that area," Gus said as he gave Ambler a shit-eating grin. "You're a busy man. I'll prescreen all of the candidates."

I smacked Gus on the arm. "Hey! You'll get him in trouble . . . yourself as well."

"I'm busy as hell; the last thing I need is a distraction," Ambler said. "I just don't have the time."

"Don't worry, you'll fit it in." Gus began to laugh hysterically.

"You're such a jerk," I said. He was bent over laughing and clutching his gut. "*He'll fit it in.* It's not *that* funny."

Ambler laughed as well. Men. Beneath the muscles

and macho, they were all just children. *Honestly!*

"Look at this," Ambler said as he tapped the window." We were several stories up. The people on the sidewalk below looked like ants.

"What are you pointing at?"

"Over there," Ambler said. He was pointing at a grassy area not far from the water.

"Is that Kowsky Plaza?"

"Correct, that's where we just came from. Now if I had been a little more vigilant, I might have seen the crime taking place."

"And if I had a crystal ball, I would have bought Apple stock years ago when it was being given away on fire sale. Shall we get to it, gentlemen, before the trail gets as cold as victim number two? I smell coffee."

"You smell coffee?" Ambler said. "Where did that come from?" Someone knocked on the door. Ambler looked through the glass panel and then waved for someone to come in. A female agent entered, carrying case files and a tray of coffee. Ambler shot me a disbelieving glance. "Come on in, Marjorie. Say hello to two of New York's finest, Detective Chalice and Detective Lido."

Marjorie set the tray down on Ambler's desk and then extended her hand. "Hi, Stephanie, I'm Marjorie Banks," she said. Banks had a sincere smile. "Herb talks about you all the time."

"Really, we hardly know each other." I tried to keep a straight face but couldn't. I chuckled. "Just kidding. Nice to meet you as well, Agent Banks."

She shook hands with Gus. "Nice to meet you," Gus said. "How long have you worked with Herb?"

"Just a few weeks. I was just reassigned from the Cleveland office." She turned to Ambler. "I made a fresh pot. I thought you might like some." She handed Ambler the case files. "These are the copy files you wanted for the detectives. Do you need anything else?"

"That's fine," Ambler said as he reached for a cup of coffee.

"Not that one," Banks said. "The one on the right has milk and sugar for you, Herb. The one in the center is black for Detective Lido and the one on the end is decaf for the expectant mother. That's right, isn't it?"

"Black is great," Gus said. "Thanks."

"Is everyone from Cleveland as nice as you? I'm going to put in for a transfer."

"Aw, she's all right," Ambler said. "A few more weeks around the New York office, and she'll be as tough as nails."

Banks blushed and then turned to Ambler. "Do you want me to stick around?"

"No. I've got it, Marjorie, but thanks for the c and c."

Banks looked puzzled for a split second. "Oh, copies and coffee . . . sure, anytime." She waved. "Nice meeting the two of you." She left and closed the door behind her.

"Nice girl," Gus said.

"Nice *girl*?" I scowled at Gus. "She's a woman first of all—what's with the girl thing?" I turned to Ambler. "She's a keeper, Herb. Don't let her get away."

"You bet," Ambler said as he pushed the two folders toward us. "You can take these with you. Let's start to talk through the case." We sat down facing him.

"Go ahead," I said. "Shoot."

"First off, I want to remind the two of you that this geographic area of Manhattan is still *and will always be* a hot zone. Your average Joe will never forget September 11, but it's not uppermost in his conscious mind. To this day, anything that happens on or around Ground Zero gets looked at under a microscope, and Kowsky Plaza is smack dab in the center of the hot zone. Nothing is routine, nothing. So if a body is found in Kowsky Plaza, it doesn't just get looked at as a routine homicide. We examine every incident as if it might have something to do with the next geopolitical event, and I am not about to allow that to happen on my watch. Are we on the same page?" Gus and I nodded. I reached for my decaf and took a sip. "The Bureau investigators are great, but they're not homicide cops, and that's why I asked Shearson to lend me my two favorite detectives." I always knew Ambler to be sharp, but he had really stepped up his game—he was acting like a leader and no longer as a field agent.

"So tell us about number one? I assume the forensic reports are in these folders. Where was the body found and did you find a similar ceramic medallion with the body?"

Ambler shook his head. "You bet." He raised his finger. "Just one minute." He picked up his phone and punched in an internal code. "We're ready for you. Come right in." Ambler hung up the phone.

I heard a hand on the doorknob. Someone entered the room. I turned and saw a face I knew very well but never expected to see. The last time I had seen this face was in the hospital. It was the face of a brilliant man who was succumbing to the ravages of brain cancer, a man that medical science expected to die. My eyes grew moist. I'm not usually this emotional, but with the pregnancy and all, my hormones were running amuck. I jumped out of my chair and threw my arms around Damien Zugg.

Chapter Seven

I gave Zugg a peck on the cheek and stepped back to take him in. He held an evidence box, which he put down on Ambler's couch. I had only known him as a frail man, a man trying desperately to cling to life. He looked far better than the last time I saw him. He didn't have the robust demeanor of a triathlete or anything even close to that, but he looked stronger and healthier. "Damien, I'm so—"

"Yeah, me too," he said. "Funny, isn't it? Everyone had me figured for dead."

Gus was standing behind me, ready to pounce on Zugg. I stepped aside and allowed the two men to embrace.

"So you're okay?" I asked.

"I got a stay of execution. I'm in a test trial for a new drug. And guess what? It's a derivative of scorpion venom." Zugg smiled from ear to ear. He had self-medicated with scorpion venom in an attempt to cure his glioma tumors—it was his Hail Mary pass, as all of his doctors had lost hope. "I'm in remission."

"That's great!" Gus bellowed.

I turned to Ambler. "You're such a shit. You couldn't tell me Damien was back? You didn't let on that you knew anything."

"I thought the surprise would be better," Ambler said.

"You're back to work for the Bureau?" I asked Zugg.

"I'm just consulting, Stephanie. I'm not ready to give

it my heart and soul yet. Herb brought me in to help on this case. I'm taking it one day at a time."

"That's just wonderful." I turned to Ambler. "So Damien will be working with us?"

Ambler nodded. "As I told you earlier this morning, I only associate myself with the right people." Zugg was a brilliant forensics man, but I couldn't believe Ambler would put him back into action. Then again, Ambler didn't know what I knew.

The last time I had seen Zugg was in the back of an ambulance. He had a criminal cornered and was reciting verses from the bible as he put an end to the felon's life. Zugg was a genius but had been struggling mentally due to the damage caused by the brain cancer. As with the cancer, had his mental instability been eradicated? Was that in remission too? During that moment when he'd cornered the felon in the back of the ambulance, I had the opportunity to stop Zugg, but I did not. His victim was a heinous individual, who was literally begging for Zugg to end his life. Zugg was terminally ill, and I thought that he was going to die—funny how things work out. My conscience reared and kicked me like a mule.

"I can't believe we're going to be working together again," Zugg said.

Me neither. "So, what's in the box? I have to solve this case before my mother throws me a baby shower."

"Same old Chalice," Zugg said. "All work." Zugg sat down on the couch and opened the evidence box. Inside the box was another tablet like the one that had been found with the victim at Kowsky Plaza. It was blue as well. The numeral one had been inlaid with human incisors. A small piece had been chipped from the corner of the tablet. Zugg took it out of the evidence box and held it up as Charlton Heston had in *The Ten*

Commandments. "Let my people go."

I understood Zugg's reference. "A religious tablet? Are we dealing with a hate crime?"

"Maybe. Possibly," Ambler said.

Gus walked up to Zugg to examine the tablet more closely. "Blue and white are the colors of the Israeli flag, aren't they?"

"Yes," I replied.

Gus touched the tablet at the lower corner where it had been chipped. "Was it damaged when you found it?"

"Is it damaged or is that the area where the lab took a sample for analysis?" I asked.

"That's right, Chalice. That's where we removed a sample for testing," Zugg said.

"So what do we know about the stone the tablet is made from?

"Oh, it's not made of stone," Ambler said.

"Then what's it made from?"

"Cement," Zugg replied.

"Anything special about that?" Gus asked.

"Indeed," Zugg said. "Cement is a mixture of limestone, clay, and sand.

"And?"

"Limestone is calcium carbonate. It's found in abundance just about everywhere on earth. It's also what bones are made of, and that's what is in this tablet. The cement is made from crushed human bones."

Chapter Eight

"**Bones**? Really? Human bones?"

"That's right," Ambler said. "Damien was able to retrieve DNA evidence from the concrete in the medallion. Good thing too, because that's all we have. A kid walked the evidence into the building. Someone paid him twenty bucks to be a messenger."

"No body?"

"No body, Chalice. The medallion is all we have."

"Can we identify a victim from the crushed bones?" Gus asked.

"Unfortunately no," Zugg said. "Human bones contain low concentrations of degraded DNA. It makes them unsuitable for nuclear DNA examination. Besides, even if nuclear examination was possible, we would have to find a match in the National Missing Person DNA Database or at the Sorenson Genealogy Foundation. That means someone would have needed to report the missing person to one of these two entities and an adequate DNA sample submitted as a reference identification standard—not the best odds."

"Then what do we have?" Gus asked.

"We were able to perform mitochondrial analysis," Zugg continued. "That kind of testing doesn't give us individual-specific information, but we were able to determine a genetic profile. You should find the information helpful to your investigation."

"Dear God, would someone please spit it out already? What did we find?"

"Well, for one thing, the DNA we found is homogeneous throughout the cement, which means that all the bones used to make it came from the same person," Zugg said. "Secondly, the Y-chromosome is present."

"That means it's male DNA," Gus volunteered.

"Correct," Ambler replied.

"Surely the DNA tells us more than that."

Zugg walked to Ambler's desk, picked up my coffee cup, and began to drink. "It does, but don't get your hopes up." He finished my coffee and turned to Ambler. "The coffee is delicious."

"Banks made a fresh pot," Ambler said.

"Marjorie made this?" Zugg asked. Ambler reaffirmed with a nod. "Oh, I like her. This is the first good cup of coffee I've had since I came back to work." He put the empty cup back on Ambler's desk.

Yeah, I thought it was good too. "I may get a cup."

My comment prompted Gus to check the cups on Ambler's desk. I could see him counting to himself, "One, two . . ." He looked at me and shrugged. I guess Zugg still has a couple of loose screws.

"Focus, people, what else does the DNA tell us?

Zugg picked up another coffee cup and returned to the couch. Just for the record, he now had Gus' coffee in his hand. He sat down and crossed his legs. "The victim's name was Cohen."

"What?"

"The victim's name was Cohen," Zugg repeated. "The YAP marker was found on the Y-Chromosome. Six specific Y-STR markers were present along with genetic material belonging to the Y-haplogroup J1c3."

"Sometimes I really wish I had completed a degree in advanced genealogy . . . but I became a cop instead. Damien, what does all this mean?"

"Long story short?"

"Yes please." *Dear God, please.*

"It means that the victim shares the same genetic signature as Aaron, the brother of Moses."

"The victim is related to Moses?" Gus asked in a disbelieving tone.

"Yes, but the same is true of almost anyone named Cohen; it's not an exclusive circle."

"So you can analyze a spec of the victim's DNA and determine his genealogy back to—"

"Approximately 1600 BC," Zugg replied. "That's when it's believed that Aaron lived. Actually, we can go back thirty or forty thousand years, but I don't think it will help your chances of capturing your unsub."

"That's incredible. This information is one-hundred-percent accurate?"

"Well no, nothing is that precise. We're going back to the Middle East almost four thousand years ago. Who knows who slept with whom? Bloodlines cross and cross and cross. I'm just telling you that the chances are pretty good that the victim's name was Cohen, but it could have been Johnson or Atkins or Limbaugh."

I laughed. Personally, a corpse named Limbaugh wouldn't bother me one bit. "Any missing person's reports on a male named Cohen, Herb? I'm sure you checked."

"You know we did," Ambler replied. "There are several of them, and we're checking into every one. The problem is that we don't know when the victim died or the victim's age. The victim could have disappeared five days ago or fifty years ago. He could have come from New Jersey or Istanbul. We would be able to determine age if we had a reasonably large portion of a formed bone, but we don't. Possible missing persons who match the victim's profile are listed in the files we gave you."

"I guess we don't know a hell of a lot."

Ambler smiled. "That's why you're here, kiddo."

Chapter Nine

"**There's** my baby!" Ma reached out and smothered me with a hug. She planted a wet one on my cheek. "You smell like a mommy-to-be."

"I smell like a mommy-to-be?" I was standing outside the door and had yet to enter her apartment—I doubt a bear's sense of smell is as acute as my mother's. "How does a pregnant woman smell?"

"Oh I don't know, you just do. Now get out of my way and let me hug Gus." Ma gave Gus the same octopus hug and kiss. "I made everything you could ever possibly want for dinner. I hope you're hungry."

"Did you ever know me not to be?"

Ma didn't answer right away—I couldn't believe that she had to think about it. "God bless you, you've always had a good appetite, but now that you're eating for two . . ." It was good to see Ma so happy. She had gone through a real rough patch after my father died—she dressed in black for a full two years after he was gone. At this moment, she looked more alive than I had seen her in years. She was alive with the expectation of becoming a grandmother. "I made lasagna and a roast. I baked a cheesecake: pineapple with a graham-cracker crust."

"Ma, even pregnant women are supposed to watch their calories."

"Bah! That's nonsense. You can eat anything you want," she said with her patented dismissive hand gesture. "Besides, knowing you, it will all go to your boobs." She smiled at Gus. "Any problems with that, handsome?" Gus appeared to be tongue-tied. "No, I didn't think so." She finally yielded her sentry post, and we walked into the apartment. "I almost forgot. I made you a little tripe."

I stopped dead in my tracks. "You made me tripe? Are you crazy?"

"You loved it as a little girl—I used to make it for your father."

I sniffed the air and wrinkled my nose. "So that's what that awful smell is." I buried my face in Gus' shoulder. "God help me, the woman is insane," I said playfully.

"It's delicious," she insisted. "You'll try it, won't you, Gus?"

"I've never heard of it," Gus said. For the record, tripe is an Italian dish. Gus' mother is Greek. BTW, her moussaka is to die for.

"It's stomach lining," I volunteered. "It's absolutely putrid."

"It can't be *that* bad," Gus said, but I could tell he was just trying to be nice. "Sure, I'll try a little."

"He's afraid to say no. Where's Ricky?" I asked.

"I sent your brother to the bakery for some fresh Italian bread. He'll be back soon."

"Gus, our baby's going to think I'm a whale."

"Don't worry, babe," Gus said. "I'll let you know the moment I spot a blowhole."

Gus' blowhole-comment made me chuckle. This was the third week in a row that Ma had invited us to dinner. The menu varied each week, but the calorie count was always in the stratosphere. "Sit down in the living room, I've got to check on the roast. Would you like a beer, Gus?" Ma asked.

"I'd love one. Thanks," he said.

"How about you, Stephanie, care for a cold one?"

"Ma, you know I can't have any alcohol."

"One beer? You can't have one little bottle of beer? It's full of vitamins."

"I take vitamins."

"It's not the same," she said. "Hops are good for you."

"No beer," I reiterated.

"Okay, I'll just bring one for Gus. You can taste his if you like." Ma walked into the kitchen.

"I'll lay you straight odds she returns with two bottles."

Gus smiled and gave me a kiss. "You've made her really happy."

"I didn't do it alone." I nuzzled his neck and whispered in his ear. "All this talk about food is making me horny."

Gus smiled and raised a pointer finger as if he were signaling for a waiter. "Check please."

"Yeah you just try. Ma will cut you off at the knees—you'll never make it to the door. You think you've seen some tough hombres on the street? They're nothing compared to my mother. You're not getting out of here until you've been stuffed like a *piñata*."

"But I want to go home and mess around."

"Not a prayer, boyfriend. By the time Ma gets finished with you, you won't have the energy to take off your socks." He sighed—alas, he knew I was right.

I heard keys in the door lock. I turned just as my brother Ricky walked through the door. He gave me a huge smile, dropped the bag of bread on the floor, and ran over to give me a hug. That was Ricky. He was a man with the mind of a child, but I loved every inch of him. He hugged me as if he hadn't seen me in years. His greeting was always the same. It was like being greeted by a Labrador retriever—unconditionally loving.

"You look great, Stephanie," he said. "Ma says you've got the glow."

"I think Ma's the one with the glow."

Ricky thought for a moment and then his face lit up. "Is Ma going to have a baby too?"

I had to bite my tongue. "No, Ricky, I just meant that she's more excited than I am."

"Yeah, she's pretty excited," Ricky said. He made an unpleasant face. "She cooked you some smelly stomach stuff. I think it's going to be bad. I asked her why she made it, and she said that you had a craving for it." He turned to Gus. "Oh hi, Gus. Ma says she loves you."

"She did?"

"Uh-huh. She said she didn't want Stephanie falling in love with a cop like she did . . . but then she met you."

Really? I looked at Gus. I wasn't sure which of us was going to cry first.

"Give me a hug," Gus said and threw his arms around Ricky. My brother had yet to master the man hug. For him, it was one size fits all.

"Am I your brother yet?" Ricky asked.

Gus looked at me, and I could see that he was getting choked up. Gus was all man. He was six foot two inches tall and built like a commando. He could throw down with anyone on the street, but at this moment, his emotions were getting the better of him. I saw his eyes glaze over. "You are indeed," he said.

I put my arms around the two of them. "This feels good," I said. "This feels really good."

Chapter Ten

As I said, Gus was all man. He polished off two portions of lasagna, a healthy slab of Ma's roast, cheesecake, and still had enough energy to put the cherry on my sundae . . . or did I put my cherry on his sundae? Either way, it was a complete evening.

Even Gus has his limits. He was sound asleep next to me while I reviewed the case files we had received in Ambler's office. It was a cop's worst nightmare. It contained page after page of laboratory analysis. I was just a layperson, and after a while, graphs that compared haplogroups, chromosomal markers, and genealogical DNA gave me a headache. There was no real evidence to sink my teeth into, no crime scene, no witnesses, no nothing. The concrete tablet in the FBI's possession had been delivered to FBI headquarters anonymously. An unidentified man wearing a hoodie and dark sunglasses had handed a kid twenty bucks to drop off an envelope at the FBI building.

I looked at the clock. It was only 10:00 p.m. I picked up the phone and dialed Ambler at home. "What's going on, G-man?"

"Is that you, Chalice?"

"Sure as shooting. Did I disturb you?"

"No. I'm doing some paperwork and watching TV."

"*Mission Impossible*?"

"Uh no."

Really? No? Ambler was in all likelihood the world's greatest fan of the original *Mission Impossible* TV show. I think he slept in Jim Phelps jammies. “I can’t believe it. What are you watching?”

“I’m embarrassed to tell you.”

“Aw, come on.”

“It’s that important for you to know?”

“Pretty please.”

“I’m watching *MANswers* on Spike TV.”

MANswers is a men’s-interests TV Show. They ask questions like: what is the best day of the year to get lucky, and which women are easier, redheads or blondes? Scantily clad women act out the answers by performing skits—the dramatizations incorporate a lot of giggling. I don’t see the show winning any kind of award, but I understood why it was popular with the gents. Ambler had no reason to be embarrassed, but I wasn’t surprised that he was. He had been like a second father to me. The idea of him watching mindless bimbo TV . . . well, I guess there was this certain level of expectation about how a father figure should behave. It didn’t matter to me because Ambler was a quality guy. We all have needs, right? “That’s okay, I’ve watched *The Green Lantern* at least ten times. I can’t get enough of Ryan Reynolds in that skin-tight plasma suit. Who am I to judge?”

“Where’s Lido?”

“I’m looking at his chiseled body right now. He’s out for the count. Say, does that man show have any ideas about this case because I sure don’t? When will we have forensics back on John Doe?”

“They haven’t been able to start. The crime lab is warming the body slowly so that it doesn’t decompose and become a hundred and fifty pounds of Jell-O. We may get some information back tomorrow.”

“You don’t give a girl much to work with—a chunk of concrete and a stack of DNA studies won’t solve a case like this."

"I never said it was going to be easy. Like I said, we should know more tomorrow. I got you out of the office, didn't I?"

"Yes, and I'm eternally grateful. We still have to find out who killed this distant relative of Aaron and Moses, and this morning's victim. If the perp fashioned these mosaic medallions, he may be an artisan or craftsman of some sort."

Gus stirred. "Who are you talking to?" he said in an adorable sleepy voice.

"I'm discussing the case with Ambler."

"Oh. Tell him I said hi." He began to snore within seconds.

"I'm going back to Kowsky Plaza in the morning. Maybe I'll get a spark of genius. Call me if the lab finds anything useful."

"You'll be the first to know. Goodnight, Stephanie."

I was about to say goodnight when a meddling idea popped into my head. "Hey, Herb, why don't you have dinner with Agent Banks?"

"Marjorie? Would you please stop playing matchmaker."

"I don't know . . . she's awfully sweet. I can definitely see her in the role of Mrs. Herbert Ambler. It beats watching *Bimbo Answers* on the Shower Material Network."

"Shouldn't you be reading up on the next trimester or something? Same old Stephanie Chalice, you just never quit. How would it look for me to be dating a subordinate? I just got the job."

I think he likes her. I didn't want to push too hard. The relationship was brand new. *Only time will tell.* "Goodnight, old friend. Sweet dreams."

Chapter Eleven

Anya Kozakova's eyes were red while she banged away on the computer keyboard late into the night. Her apartment was swelteringly hot from too much steam heat, and her neighbors were having sex for the third time that evening.

"Animals," she screamed in her heavy Russian accent. "Practice some self-control."

She worked at a long table with computers and processing devices from end to end—when all of the equipment was running, it threw off enough energy to heat a North Sea oil rig. To make matters worse, the old radiator beneath the table whistled like a teakettle, and the shutoff valve had been broken off. It was in the low forties outside, but the temperature in her apartment was over eighty. She kicked the radiator with her foot. "Such a waste of money," she complained.

She entered a few final commands and then waited for the processor to catch up with her instructions. "Finished. Finally." Her stomach rumbled. Her cotton blouse was unbuttoned. She looked down at her exposed midriff and saw her stomach muscles undulate. She stamped out her cigarette in an ashtray, walked over to the thirty-year-old Frigidaire refrigerator, and opened the door. A plate of cherry blintzes was covered with Saran Wrap. She picked one of them up with her hand and ate it while she walked around the small apartment. She was licking the sticky cherry filling off of her fingers when someone knocked on her door.

"Who the fuck is that?" She wondered if her neighbor was drunk enough to confront her, but then she heard two successive grunting sounds coming from their apartment, confirming that they were still in bed . . . or perhaps on the kitchen table.

She tied the bottom of her blouse into a knot to somewhat cover her bra. She unlocked the door and opened it without checking to see who was there.

Marat Vetrov stood on the other side of the door holding a paper bag. "You don't ask who it is? What if I was here to rob you?"

"I'm not afraid. Besides, I can kick your ass." Anya was a strong woman with muscular shoulders and arms.

"You look very intimidating with jelly on your face." Vetrov was a giant. He was thick and round. His face was covered with black stubble. His accent was heavy Russian, like Kozakova's.

"So?"

"You're eating week-old blintzes?" he said.

"What's wrong with them?"

"Yeech." He made a sour face. "You're going to kill yourself with the shit you eat. You don't know how to cook?" He pushed past her and set the paper bag down on the kitchen table. "Pastrami sandwiches. You think you can make some coffee?" The sounds coming from her neighbor's apartment grew louder. "What the hell is that? The Russian fleet is in?"

"They fuck all day and night. I think they're taking some kind of love potion. I've never heard anything like it." Kozakova locked the door and turned toward Vetrov. She rubbed her eyes. The knot at the bottom of her blouse opened, revealing her bra and ample cleavage.

Vetrov winked at her. "It doesn't give you ideas?"

"I'm writing computer code at two o'clock in the morning. You think this makes me think of sex?"

"Apparently nothing makes you think of sex. You exercise and you write computer code. As far as I've seen, you have no other interests."

"I'm disciplined." She began to re-tie the knot in her blouse and then stopped. "I'm not worried about being modest. It's too hot in here. The landlord is an idiot—the heat is on twenty-four hours a day." She took two glasses out of the kitchen cabinet and filled them with instant coffee and hot tap water.

"You have to boil it, moron," Vetrov said in disgust. He spilled the two glasses of coffee into the sink. "Let me do it. Eat your sandwich. I just came from the all-night deli; it's still warm."

Kozakova sat down without hesitation. She had the sandwich unwrapped and in her mouth in seconds. "You're a good friend, Marat," she said while she chewed. "Don't think for a moment that we're going to bed. I'm too tired." The volume of her neighbor's love noises had built to an earsplitting crescendo. "I've got to find a new apartment."

"How's the pastrami?"

"Stringy, but tasty."

Vetrov opened the refrigerator. He examined the plate of blintzes and then threw them into the trash. "You're welcome."

Kozakova heard the sound of something falling into the trashcan, but wasn't paying attention. She was thinking about the program she had just written and was relieved to be finished with illegal work. "For what?" She finally turned and looked into the trashcan. "You threw out the blintzes? I just had one—they're still good."

"You're hopeless." He stared at the dented saucepan he was going to use to boil water. "I don't have the patience for this. Have you got some vodka?"

"Vodka I have." She stood and walked to the cabinet. She returned with a full bottle of Putinka Vodka.

Vetrov's eyes sparkled. "Putinka? *Very nice.* Where did you get that?"

"I buy it online. I can't drink the crap they sell in the American liquor stores." Kozakova broke the seal and poured half a glass for each of them. She lifted her glass and toasted, *"Budem zdorovy."*

"Yes, he concurred. "Good health." He took a big swallow and savored the vodka as it coated his tongue and ran down his throat. "This is heaven. It's expensive?"

"Expensive? No. It's half the price of that goose shit everyone else drinks."

"So what were you working on?"

"Security codes."

"What kind of security codes?"

"Better you don't know."

"You're such a bitch. Who brings you meals when you're locked away in your apartment like a slave all night?"

Kozakova gnawed through the pastrami sandwich as if it were kindling being fed through a wood chipper. She looked at him pointedly. "If I don't tell you, it's for your own good."

"Yeah, fuck you, Anya."

She finished the last bite of her sandwich and drained the contents of her glass. "Don't make such a sad face. I changed my mind; I'll give you sex." She stood and walked behind Vetrov. She caressed his neck with her long fingernails. "You showered today?"

He cursed her with his eyes. "Of course I showered. You think I'm an animal?"

"Give me a minute, sexy man, I'll go wash up."

Vetrov waited until he heard the bathroom door close

before he jumped out his chair. The computer screen was still filled with code. He inserted a flash drive into the USB port and copied Kozakova's program. He was not her intellectual equal, but like her, he was an engineer. Alone, back in the solitude of his apartment, he would be able to decipher her genius and make it work to his advantage. He withdrew the flash drive just as the bathroom door latch clicked open.

"I'm ready," Kozakova called to him. "Come into the bedroom, Marat, and bring the vodka."

He slipped the flash drive into his back pocket and buttoned it for good measure. He picked up the vodka bottle and took another drink. He felt himself stir as he swaggered toward her bedroom.

Chapter Twelve

I woke up in a great mood. I was happy. As was recently the case, I was ravenous. Brilliant sunshine streamed through the window, and my lover was lying next to me in bed. The air was filled with the wonderful aroma of Ma's sauce. They're not kidding about the appetite thing. I was in my fourth month, and my hormones were out of control. I felt as if I could eat twenty-four hours a day. I still could not understand why I didn't weigh three hundred pounds. *God is good, my friends. God is good.*

It dawned on me (right after I drooled from the aroma of Ma's sauce) that I didn't live at home with my mother any longer. Ma's sauce had an incredible bouquet. I can still remember standing in the kitchen as a child and marveling at the incredible food that she was preparing. It was impossible to forget.

But if Ma wasn't in the kitchen, who was?

I pulled back the sheets. "Huh?" I was wearing a red apron and . . . well, that was about it. I looked around for my slippers, but they were missing. In their place was a pair of cherry red pumps. This was not a modest pair of shoes. They had platforms and spike heels. They were man-killer shoes, the kind a woman wore when she had romance on her mind. I checked the label—they were Manolo Blahnicks. Wow, this really was an outstanding morning.

I slipped into them and stood up. I examined myself in the mirror. The apron covered my baby bump, but boobs and ass were poking out everywhere. I checked to make sure that Gus was still asleep. He was. *Idiot,* I thought, *do you have any idea what you're missing?* Gus was definitely going to be mad when he learned what he had missed. I was dressed for one thing and one thing only, but as mentioned, the Hunger God was in command, so instead of jumping on Gus and riding him like a thoroughbred at the Belmont Stakes, I spun on those spike heels and made a beeline for the kitchen.

"Ma? What are you doing here?" My mother was at the kitchen counter. She looked just as I remembered her when I was a little girl. She was grating Romano cheese. She turned to me with a big smile on her face, wiped her hands on a kitchen towel, and ladled a spoon of sauce from the pot.

"Taste it, my beautiful, pregnant girl." She held the sauce under my nose for a moment and allowed the aroma to waft through my nostrils. The aroma was exquisite—my knees began to buckle. I couldn't wait any longer. I opened my mouth and tasted it. The flavor of Ma's sauce was so incredibly delicious. I let it sit on my tongue, savoring every incredible nuance: the sweetness and the perfectly seasoned goodness.

"Oh my God, it's *so* good."

Ma pointed to a loaf of Italian bread. I tore off a chunk, dipped it in the sauce, and stuffed it into my mouth. *Jesus, I think I just had an orgasm.* I had sauce all over my face. I looked like an infant who had just attempted to feed itself for the first time.

"That's it, enjoy, honey," Ma said. *"Mangia."* She smiled robustly. "By the way, Stephanie, what the hell are you wearing?"

"I don't know." I was too busy stuffing my face with fresh bread and sauce to care. "Ma, you still make the best sauce in the world. I don't know if I'll ever be able to cook as well as you do."

"No worries, child," she said, looking me up and down. "With a body like that you can order take out. I don't think Gus will mind."

Sauce dripped into my cleavage. "Oh Christ, look at me. I look like a pig." I looked up with a silly grin on my face. "Ma?" Ma was gone.

I looked around. Gus was standing at the counter behind me. He was naked and wrist-deep in chop meat. He was forming a meatball and smiling a devilish smile.

He motioned for me to come closer. "I'll show you how to cook."

"Like that? No way. Put your boxers on."

He extended his chop-meat-encrusted hand toward me. "We all have our methods. Come on. It will be fun." I got closer. He gave me a little kiss on the lips.

"You understand that we can't serve this food to anyone else."

He looked around and shrugged. "I don't see anyone from the Board of Health, do you?"

"You'd better be careful before you dip your salami in that sauce."

"My salami is just fine."

Oh God . . . yes, I know. "All right. You win," I said, capitulating. "What do you want me to do?"

Gus didn't respond with words. He poured olive oil on my hands and began to gently massage them until my hands were completely coated.

"What are you doing?"

"Shhh. You have to lubricate your hands if you want to do a good job on the balls. It's my trade secret."

I laughed so hard that I snorted. He worked my hands firmly, applying pressure, and working olive oil around my fingers and joints. *That feels so good.* "Hey, this isn't one of your perverse little fantasies, is it?

Because there's no way that I'm going to play choke the chicken next to all this fresh produce."

"You really are nuts." Gus laughed and began to work the olive oil around my wrists and up my arms. I closed my eyes and embraced his touch.

"You're one hell of a cook, Gus Lido." His hands were up around my shoulders. He began to massage the back of my neck.

"Okay," he said. "Get in front of me and put your hands in the chop meat."

Really? I'm all hot and bothered. He expects me to cook? Now? I felt Gus' warm breath on my neck as he stepped behind me and put his arms around me. "Hey, is that a *braciole* in your pocket or are you just happy to see me?"

He laughed. "I'm not even standing at attention."

God bless him, *he wasn't.*

"Cook," he commanded. I felt his warm, oil-covered hands under my apron, massaging my belly. "I love you. I can't believe that we're going to have a baby together." He kissed me on the neck. I felt him nuzzling my cheek.

I felt warm and tingly all over. My body went limp in his arms. "Take me back to bed. I don't think I have the strength to stand." I turned and kissed him full on the lips.

"You are in bed."

"What?"

"You are in bed."

My eyes snapped open. I was in still in bed and covered to the neck with the comforter. I was drenched in sweat and my heart was pounding. "You mean that I was—"

"You were dreaming, Stephanie."

Oh damn! "It felt so real."

I had always been a notoriously vivid dreamer, but

since becoming pregnant . . . oh dear Lord, my hormones were just running amuck. My dreams were even more intense and vivid. I had actually thought that I tasted Ma's sauce, and I had been absolutely sure that I felt Gus' muscular hands on me as he massaged my shoulders and neck. *God, dreams can be such a tease.*

I pushed back the covers and began fanning myself with my hands. "I'm burning up."

Gus leaned over me and gently blew air on my neck. "Is there anything I can do for you?" he said in an affectionate tone.

I looked up at his handsome face and realized that dreams may tease at times, but they can also provide a preview of reality.

"Two things," I said. "Make love to me and then take me out for breakfast."

Chapter Thirteen

Nick Sonellio strolled out onto the deck of his Staten Island home, put both hands on the redwood railing, and looked out at his backyard. The quarter-acre parcel was bordered on all sides by a white-picket fence that he had installed himself using a post-hole digger and his own two hands. The fence had held up for more than fifteen years.

His wife Toni followed him out to the deck and placed her arms around his waist. "Come here, skinny," she said, as she pulled him closer. He was still staring out at the yard as she examined his face adoringly.

"So what do you think?" he asked.

"Still handsome," Toni replied. "You're still my Nick."

"That's not what I meant."

"Then what do you mean?"

Sonellio turned to his wife of forty years and then glanced through the kitchen window at the oxygen tank on the floor. She followed his gaze. "Do you think I'll make it through the summer?" he asked.

"Yes," she stated emphatically, ". . . and well past. Don't be so gloomy. The oxygen is just there in case you need it. Have you used it so far?" She looked into his eyes beseechingly, already certain of his response.

"No."

"So forget it's even there. What do you want for breakfast? I went to the store and filled the refrigerator before you woke up."

He smiled at her tenderly and gave her a small kiss

on the lips. "Nothing heavy, maybe toast and orange juice."

"Coming right up."

"I'll give you a hand."

"Nonsense." She gave him a smack on the behind. "Sit your keister down and breathe in some of that fresh Staten Island air." She inhaled theatrically. "I think I can smell the kills today."

Sonellio laughed. "I can't believe we had to come home from Maine—now that was fresh air."

"Maine? Who needs it? That was your dream, not mine. How long did you think I could clean trout and swat mosquitoes before I went absolutely bananas? We're better off here, close to people we know." She was still looking into his eyes when her courage failed. A tear formed in the corner of her eye. She pulled him close again. "You want to be near friends, don't you?"

Sonellio was tougher than his wife. He smiled for her benefit. "Sure, they're okay," he quipped. "So, are you going to make me breakfast or what?"

"All right, I'm nothing more than a short-order cook around here anyway," she said lightheartedly. She rubbed the tip of her nose against his. "Give me five minutes. I'll rustle up your chow."

Sonellio followed his wife's instructions. He filled his lungs with fresh air, even though it was painful to do so. He didn't care how much Staten Island's landfill smelled. He would have given anything to be able to breathe as he used to. Every breath was a reminder of how foolish he had been for smoking since he was a teen.

He scanned the white picket fence and pictured himself pounding the posts into the ground. It was a grueling job that had taken an entire weekend. He was proud to see that his handiwork had endured. *Even if I won't,* he mused. He sat down on a lounge chair. He inadvertently caught a glimpse of the green oxygen tank in the kitchen. "Damn." *I'll be up there with you soon, Frank.*

Frank Chalice was one of Sonellio's closest friends and had been the best detective under his command until he lost his battle with diabetes. "Your kid's doing you proud, Frank. The apple didn't fall far from the tree."

"Who the hell are you talking to out here," Toni said. "Do I have to worry that there's something wrong with your mind also?" She handed him a glass of orange juice. "Here, freshly squeezed . . . by migrant farmers in Chile."

Sonellio looked at his wife with a sheepish expression. "I was just thinking about Frank Chalice. Do you believe he's gone almost five years?"

Toni frowned momentarily and then hoisted a huge grin. "Don't go getting all gloomy on me, okay?"

He stroked her cheek. "He was a good friend. I miss him. I miss his kid too. I haven't seen her in months."

"Stephanie? I like that girl; she's a real pistol. Why don't you invite her out? The secret's out of the bag, isn't it? Didn't you tell me that she declared her relationship with Gus Lido?"

"Sure," he laughed, "Right after she got pregnant."

"What are you going to do? Things are different today. Do you remember how we had to sneak around when we were dating? My mother would have killed me if she knew what was going on. Remember the time you gave me a hickie and I had to wear a turtleneck in July?"

"We had some good times, didn't we?"

"Good times, my ass—I had to convince my mother that it was fashionable. I paid my best friend ten bucks to stop by the house wearing a turtleneck just to sell my story."

"I remember. That was so funny."

"So . . . are you going to call her?" He shrugged. "Stop hemming and hawing."

"But—"

"But what, she doesn't know that you've got cancer? She's a detective for God's sake—and a good one, according to you. I think she'd be pretty pissed off if you didn't tell her."

"She doesn't even know that I'm back. She thinks I'm still up at the cabin."

Toni reached for his phone case and took out his cell phone. "If it's called a smartphone, how come it doesn't make you smart?" She tapped it lightly against his forehead. "Whether you're here another week or another ten years . . . the people who love you have a right to know. Now I haven't been slaving over a hot toaster for the past thirty seconds for nothing. Your breakfast is getting cold."

Sonellio nodded and took the phone from his wife. "How come *you're* so smart?"

"*Someone* has to take care of you."

Sonellio took a sip of orange juice and turned to follow his wife into the house. As he did, he noticed a piece of torn cloth caught in between the pickets of his fence. *Now what the hell is that?* "I'll be right there," he said. He put down the glass of orange juice and went down the stairs to investigate.

Chapter Fourteen

"**Michael**, come in, come in," Dr. Schrader said. He stepped aside to permit Michael Tillerman to enter his office from the waiting room. Schrader had a small psychiatric practice. His waiting room and office were tiny. The waiting room consisted of two chairs and a magazine stand. His office wasn't much bigger. He shook hands with Tillerman and gestured to one of the two available chairs at his desk. "Make yourself comfortable."

How can anyone get comfortable? Your office stinks from pipe smoke. Tillerman smiled to mask his true feelings. "Good to see you, Dr. Schrader." He wriggled in order to squeeze his enormous body into the narrow chair. He looked around and noticed that the paint had yellowed from the pipe smoke.

Schrader sat down and tapped the burnt tobacco from his pipe into the ashtray. "I can't believe how big you've gotten. Still working out at the gym?"

"Religiously."

"I'm glad the exercise agrees with you. I always recommend it. The mind heals itself in mysterious ways. If the gym works for you, stay with it, but if you get any bigger I may have to get a bigger office." Schrader chuckled. Tillerman smiled because it was the expected response.

"You're not using steroids, are you?"

"Nothing." *Nothing I need a prescription for, anyway.*

"Good, because they can cause profound mood

swings. You don't need that right now, do you?"

"Definitely not."

"Still, I don't think you were anywhere near this big the last time I saw you."

"I don't think I've changed that much."

"I guess I could be wrong. So how are you feeling, Michael?"

"I feel great." *Isn't that what you want to hear?*

Schrader opened his file and made a notation. "I'm so very pleased that I was able to get you on the Repressor test trial. It was the last medicinal option open to us. You didn't respond to Prozac, Zoloft, or Lexapro." He made an additional notation in his file. "If you didn't respond to Repressor, I would have suggested electroconvulsive therapy, which is not without risk and involves hospitalization. I'm thrilled that you've turned the corner." Schrader flipped the page. "Let's get to the test study questions, shall we?"

If I have no choice. "Sure."

"Great. On a scale of one to five, with one being poor and five being great, how would you rate your mood overall?"

"Five."

Schrader marked down Tillerman's response. "Answer *yes* or *no* or *sometimes* for each of the following: Do you feel slow or sluggish?"

"No."

"Are you able to concentrate?"

"Yes." *I can concentrate on snapping your neck like a twig.*

"Does the future seem hopeless?"

I'll say "sometimes" because I can't give a perfect answer to every question. "Sometimes."

Schrader looked up from the file. "Tell me about that. When do you feel that the future is hopeless?"

"When I think about my family."

Schrader gave Tillerman a sympathetic smile. "That's only natural. It has to be tremendously difficult to go on after suffering a tragedy like you have. The medication and therapy are not silver bullets. What happened to you and your family is terrible. There isn't a living soul who wouldn't feel blue from remembering those events. Kudos to you—you're a survivor!"

Yeah, kudos to me. My wife and two sons are dead—I'm so fucking lucky. "Thanks, doctor."

Schrader asked several additional survey questions. Tillerman responded as he felt he was expected to, reporting mostly positive results but not so positive as to appear unrealistic. When the survey was completed, Schrader opened his desk drawer and took out a sealed bottle of tablets. He recorded the control number on the survey sheet. He was about to hand the bottle to Tillerman and then paused. "Before I give this medication to you, I have to mention that you cannot continue to postpone your appointments. These pharmaceutical companies spend a fortune on the research and development of these drugs, and they only have a ten-year window to reap the rewards once they receive FDA approval. Vicor is fanatical about recordkeeping, and they've already sent a warning—they'll remove you from the test trial if you continue to miss your appointments. Do you understand, Michael? It would be a shame if that happened, especially now that you're doing so well."

Yeah, I'll be a good little guinea pig. "I try, doctor, I really do, but I have good days and bad. You understand?"

Schrader gave Tillerman an all-knowing smile and then sighed. "Let's just try to do a little better. You've been on the trial medication for almost a year now. If

Vicor gives you a final warning they'll cut you off with one last thirty-day dosage, just enough so that you can wean off the drug. After that we would have to find a replacement medication. I'm not optimistic that we'll find a suitable substitution."

"I'll try harder, doctor, I really will."

"Great. That will make life easier for both of us." He handed the bottle of tablets to Tillerman. "Here you go; your next ninety-day supply."

Oh thank God—another five minutes and I would have reached across the desk and broken your neck. "Thank you."

"Now remember, just one pill per day."

"Absolutely." *I'm up to four pills a day. Ninety tablets should last a few weeks.* Tillerman had squirreled away the tablets for months before first deciding to try them. One per day made him feel better. Four per day made him feel great. He stashed the pills in his jacket pocket and then squeezed his right wrist with his left hand to mask the powerful tremor that was building in his hand. The tremors had only begun recently—a side effect of the medication, he presumed, like the phenomenal muscle development and the inexhaustible energy. His heart began to pound as it routinely did following the hand tremor. In a moment, he would begin to sweat furiously. He saw that Schrader was eyeing his pouch of pipe tobacco. *I've got to get the hell out of here.* "All through, doctor?"

Schrader was just about to stuff fresh tobacco into his pipe. He paused, stood, and extended his hand. "Good work, Michael. Keep it up, and I'll see you for your next appointment." He warned him by shaking his finger. "Not a day later."

Tillerman smiled. "Not a day later," he agreed. He felt Schrader's puny hand in his mighty grip and fought the overwhelming urge to break every bone with one powerful squeeze.

Chapter Fifteen

"**I** can't believe how good that smells." We were walking past a sidewalk vendor in lower Manhattan. He was roasting pralines, and there was no escape from the sugary smell of roasted nuts.

"You can't be hungry again," Gus said in disbelief.

"No, *you* can't be hungry again, but as for your progeny and me, we're starving."

"You just wolfed down a huge breakfast."

He was accurate—I had just polished off poached eggs and a short stack of pancakes. Be that as it may, mom and baby were not quite satisfied. "And your point is what?"

"You're serious?"

"This detective doesn't fool around when it comes to food. I'm going to buy a bag of nuts." Gus looked dumbfounded as I walked toward the vendor's cart. My conscience was saying, "You don't need this," but the fragrance of warm, sugary pralines was wafting through my nostrils and pulling me toward the cart. It was almost as if I was under a spell and did not possess free will . . . well, not enough free will for me to turn down the pralines. I walked back to Gus, pralines in hand. I held the bag under his nose. "Do you believe how good these smell?" I popped one into my mouth. "Oh, that's heaven."

"You're going to give birth to a baby sumo wrestler."

"A sumo, you say?" I popped another praline into my mouth and crunched down. *That is so good.* "I'll love it just the same." I held out the bag so that Gus could share in the feast. "Eat some, Obi Wan Kenobi, you're our only hope. The more you eat, the less I can eat."

"I don't want to deprive the mother of my child."

I glared at him. "Stop waffling, Gus—you want me to eat or you don't want me to eat, which is it?"

"Enjoy yourself," he chuckled. "We're just a block from yesterday's crime scene. Maybe a little case crime will keep your mind off your stomach."

"It's worth a shot. Lead on McDuff," I said while I chewed on a mouthful of roasted goodness.

The autopsy of John Doe was still a work in progress. The body was still thawing, and thus, we were still waiting for the coroner's report. Nonetheless, I wanted to canvas the area to see if anything might fall into place.

We were back at Kowsky Plaza in the spot where John Doe had been found. The area was still blocked off with police tape, but there were no officers present. All there was to see was the slab of concrete with the ridiculous painting from the Berlin Wall. The area did not have video surveillance cameras. I was hoping for a moment of inspiration, a flicker of genius that would give me some direction in the case.

All of a sudden, I felt something brush by my leg. I looked down and saw an adorable little dog. It was standing on its hind legs, wagging its tail, and staring at my bag of pralines. It was on one of those long retractable leashes. "And who is this?"

"Sorry, sorry." A good-looking young man with a shaved head raced over to save us from the menacing dog at the end of the leash. "Sorry," he repeated. "She must have smelled your nuts."

Not a problem a woman usually encounters. "No worries," I said. "What's her name?"

"Pumpkin," he said. He seemed kind of bashful.

I bent over to pet the dog. "Can I give her one?"

"Oh no, please don't. Pumpkin has a sensitive stomach." He reached into his pocket and took out a biscuit. "You can give her one of these if you like."

"Sure. Thanks." Pumpkin wasn't the first dog I'd noticed in Kowsky Plaza. Kowsky Plaza housed a very cool dog run. I decided to play a hunch while Pumpkin nibbled from my hand. "Do you walk Pumpkin here every day?"

"When the weather is good," he said.

"What about in the morning?"

"Are you a cop or something?" the young man asked. He seemed intrigued by the possibility.

"Yes, we're both police officers. A body was found here yesterday morning, and we're hoping that someone might have witnessed the event."

"Really, you're cops? That's so cool." He extended his hand. "My name's Scott. I took the police exam last month."

"That's fantastic," Gus said. "How'd you do?"

"I was number fifty."

"That's pretty good. Upwards of a thousand take the exam every year. I'm sure that you'll get called." Gus turned to me. "I think he finished higher than you did, Stephanie."

The truth was that no one finished higher than I did. I was number one the year I took the exam, but I kept it quiet—humility goes a long way in the police department. "Yeah, I think you beat me, Scott. So tell me, do you walk Pumpkin early in the morning?"

"No. I just take care of her during the day. Her owner walks her in the morning."

All right, it was worth a shot. I had the right idea but the wrong dog walker. I would ask to have officers assigned to interview dog owners in the early morning when there was a chance one of them saw John Doe being deposited at the base of the ugly Berlin wall.

"Sorry," Scott continued." He seemed genuinely disappointed. "I've been walking dogs in this area since before it was renamed. It's always nice and quiet here—hardly any traffic."

Hardly any traffic—hence, a good location for the disposal of a body. I turned to Gus. "Did you know this park was renamed?"

"No," Gus said. "What was it called originally?"

Scott's eyes gleamed. "They used to call this Pumphouse Park. It was built over the old World Trade Center pumping station."

"Pumping station?" Gus asked.

"It was part of the cooling system for the towers. Chilled water from the Hudson River was originally used to cool the World Trade Center."

Chilled water? Cold enough to freeze a body? I turned to Gus and saw that we were on the same page. Scott saw from our expressions that his contribution had helped us in some manner. Poor Pumpkin had finished her biscuit and was tugging on the end of her leash. I handed Scott a business card. "Let me know if you get a call from NYPD, Scott. I have the feeling you'd make a really good cop."

Chapter Sixteen

"**As** you can see, Roger, some of the equipment is pretty worn out." Brynn Francis was the manager of the DPP Gym—a no frills gym, which was frequented by serious body builders. DPP was a bodybuilder's term. It stood for: *discipline, persistence,* and *patience.* She was giving a tour to Roger Gout, the new Staten Island regional manager.

Gout took a closer look at the weight machine, despite the fact that there was absolutely no budget for new gym equipment. He rubbed the rusted metal with his fingers. "Yeah, looks pretty old. Have you asked for a replacement machine?"

"Almost every day for the past six months. What's going on over at corporate?" Brynn asked.

"It's no secret, Brynn; we're hoping for a takeover. Bare bones gyms like this are a thing of the past. We need an infusion of money so that we can remodel all the facilities, upgrade our clientele, and raise membership fees. Just how long do you think we can go on charging ten bucks a month?"

"Anyone looking at us?"

"We're hoping for a deal with Solstice Zone. They're loaded with cash."

"Not Solstice, that's a pansy-ass gym."

"A pansy-ass gym beats an out-of-business gym any day of the week. You're one of the lucky ones. You've got a ton of square footage here, which is what Solstice looks for. They'll put in a sauna, a track, and a pool . . .

a childcare center for the working parents too. A lot of the smaller locations will probably get shut down." Gout turned suddenly at the sound of weights crashing to the floor. "What the hell is that?"

Brynn chuckled. "That's Tillerman." She pointed to the far end of the gym where a solitary bodybuilder stood over a massive barbell. "He's here every day."

Gout's eyes widened while he assessed Tillerman's size. "Christ, that guy's an animal. Is he a pro?"

"Tillerman, a pro? No. He just loves to work out. He'll be here all day. When he's done with the weight-training, he'll run on the treadmill for two hours."

"Did I say animal? What I meant to say is beast. That guy is a beast."

"That's the kind of clientele we draw: construction workers, pro bodybuilders, and sanitation workers—guys who have their afternoons free. We even have a couple of members who are legitimate wise guys."

Gout stared at Brynn. "You mean wise guys as in mobsters?"

Brynn shrugged. "It's Staten Island, isn't it?"

"Really, you've got mobsters working out here as big as this guy?" Gout seemed to shudder at the thought.

"Almost. Although Tillerman is probably the biggest guy in the gym. He's got limitless energy—he's a real specimen."

"What does he do?"

"He's got some kind of night security job—works all night and works out all day long. I haven't figured out when he sleeps. I'll introduce you. You're the new regional manager, you should meet some of the regular members."

"Uh okay," Gout said hesitantly. "He's not crazy, is he?"

"*Everyone* in here is a little over the edge. Normal

people don't work their bodies this hard. Just don't ask personal questions; he doesn't respond well."

"Whatever you say."

"Come on, follow me."

It took Gout a moment to get his feet going. It was the motion of Brynn's rear end in skintight Lycra workout pants that provided the necessary catalyst.

Tillerman was on his fifth set of a twenty-five-rep superset when Brynn and Gout approached. He ignored them completely until he had completed the set. He allowed the barbell to crash to the floor when he was done. The entire gym shook.

"Well, I guess the foundation is solid," Gout chuckled and then offered his hand to Tillerman. "Roger Gout, I'm the new regional manager."

"Gout?" Tillerman asked. "Isn't that a foot condition?"

Brynn laughed. "Mike, this is my new boss. Say hello, will you?"

The veins on Tillerman's arms were as thick as marine ropes. His hands were the size of catcher's mitts. He took Gout's hand, engulfing it in his own. "This gym is a shithouse, Mr. Gout. Everything is covered in rust."

"We're working on that, Mike. We're going to replace everything. We'll bring in all brand new state-of-the-art equipment."

"Don't change anything!" Tillerman said. "I like rust. I'd feel bad about smashing up new equipment."

"How big do you want to get? You're already huge," Gout said.

"I work out until I'm tired." Tillerman said. "It's the only way I can sleep."

"Really? Why don't you talk to a doctor about that?" Gout said.

Tillerman's eyes glazed over. "I've already talked to a

doctor." He squatted, lifted the massive barbell and hoisted it over his head. *My family is dead.* "He wasn't any help." Tillerman began to count reps as he pushed the barbell over his head, over and over again. *Doctors can't bring back the dead.* "Eleven, twelve . . ."

"Medication didn't help?" Gout asked.

"No. Eighteen, nineteen . . ."

Brynn was a small girl with an expertly crafted, athletic body. She had seen Tillerman work out a hundred times before, but the intensity with which he pressed the weights today frightened her. She stepped back and motioned for Gout to do the same. "Watch your form, Mike. You don't want to strain yourself."

The word strain did not have a place in Tillerman's vocabulary. His libido was driven by pure rage and a neurochemical cocktail that allowed him to push himself well beyond normal human limits. His pace quickened with every repetition. He drove the weights harder and faster. "Twenty-eight, twenty-nine . . ."

"That's enough, Mike. You'll hurt yourself."

Tillerman was oblivious to the warning. "Thirty-two, thirty-three . . ."

The expression on Gout's face read, *He's nuts!*

"Mike stop, you're killing yourself," Brynn warned.

"Thirty-six, thirty-seven . . ." The machine finally began to slow, and then without warning, Tillerman cast the huge barbell away. The weights crashed to the floor with such force that Brynn lost her balance from the vibration. Tillerman bent over and clutched his stomach. He panted like a racehorse that had been ridden too hard.

Brynn ran to the front counter and returned with a bottle of water. "Here, Mike. Drink!"

Tillerman squeezed the sports bottle until it was empty—twenty-four ounces of water disappeared down his throat. He crushed the plastic bottle as if he were crumpling a tissue.

"You're only human, Mike. You can't do that," Brynn said.

"I can do it," Tillerman said. "I must do it." *I miss my family.* He looked Brynn in the eye. "I'm already doing it." He sucked in enough air to create a vacuum in the gym, exhaled, and walked away.

Chapter Seventeen

Gus and I were waiting for a representative of the Port Authority of New York and New Jersey to join us so that we could take a tour of the old World Trade Center pumping station, which we had learned was located right below Kowsky Plaza, a.k.a. Pumphouse Park.

New York may have had top billing, but the Port Authority offices were located in Jersey City, New Jersey. I checked my watch. "What do you think is keeping him? It's only a twenty-minute ride."

"It's never easy getting through the Holland Tunnel—it doesn't matter what time of day it is; it's always congested."

It wasn't the nicest day. The sky was overcast, and the wind was brisk. I was dressed in a cotton blazer and slacks. The cotton jacket had become my maternity uniform because it hid my baby bump and was lightweight. Today, though the weather was raw, and I felt chilled. I wondered how cold it was down in the pumping station? Just then the wind picked up. "Oh Christ, I have to pee."

I saw Gus looking around just as the Port Authority vehicle pulled up to the curb. He was scouting for a potty. "There's a deli across the street. Run over and use the bathroom."

I scoped it out and decided from its appearance that it didn't house the kind of restroom facility I would care to use. "Don't worry, I'll hold it."

"Are you sure?"

"Completely."

"You can do one of your patented hover-squats."

"Fuhgeddaboudit!"

The Port Authority officer got out of the car. He was an elderly, black gent with rich, dark skin and white hair. "Kevin Charles," he said as he greeted us. "Chalice and Lido?"

"That be us," I said. "Thanks for the assist."

"So what's going on?" Charles asked. "You're investigating a homicide?"

"A body was found here yesterday morning," Gus said. "It was frozen solid."

"And you think it was frozen down at the pumping station? I have to tell you, that's a real long shot. The pumping station is being renovated for the new World Trade Center complex."

"So it's not operational?" I asked.

"Oh, it's operational, but with all the engineers and workers going in and out, I don't see how someone could hide a body down there long enough for it to freeze and then bring it up to the street without being seen."

"But it's cold enough down there to freeze a body?"

"The river water is cold as fuck, but it's not a refrigeration plant." Charles scratched his head. "There's frost on the inlet pipes all the time—I suppose it's possible."

"So you don't mind if we poke around?" I asked.

"Hell, you got me out of the office—poke around as long as you like." Charles locked his car. "All right, let's take a walk."

"Tell us about the pumping station. I'm curious."

Charles squeezed in between us while we walked to the pumping station street entrance. "Originally, the entire World Trade Center complex was cooled with water from the Hudson."

"The water's that cold?" Gus asked.

"Hell yes. The water doesn't get pulled from the surface; it gets pulled from down deep, and it's freezing cold—well below thirty-two degrees this time of year. It doesn't freeze because it's always moving and because of the mineral content—if you don't believe me, go take a dip."

"A dip in the Hudson? No way, it's like one big festering sore. Everyone knows the Hudson is polluted."

"Uh yeah, that's one of the reasons the pumping station is going to be modified, to have less of an environmental impact. The old system used to pull as much as a hundred and twenty thousand gallons per minute."

"Sounds like a shitload of water," Gus said. "It doesn't sound like a system like that would have much trouble freezing one little body."

"Probably not," Charles replied, "but there are a hell of a lot easier ways to freeze a body. I know the meat-packing district isn't what it used to be, but there are still some slaughterhouses in operation, and there's tons of meat in deep freeze at all times. Easier to hide a body in with all that beef than it is to get it in and out of the pumping station."

"I'm surprised the pumping station wasn't destroyed in the September 11 attack."

"It's right here beneath the park, not beneath the World Trade Center site. The intake, pump station, underground piping, and discharge station are still intact and will be used to cool parts of the new complex that's being built."

"But not all of it?" Gus asked.

"No. River water will cool the Performing Arts Center, Education Center, and the Memorial Center, but the Freedom Tower will be cooled with a new state-of-the-art system."

We came upon the entrance to the pumping station. We entered to find a security guard dozing at his post.

Charles produced a fake cough. The guard roused slowly. He didn't seem embarrassed to have been caught asleep. Charles flashed his credentials. "Busy?" Charles asked, unable to conceal the chuckle he was trying to suppress.

The security guard took a sip from a water bottle. "You're the first visitors I've had all day. Everyone's on strike again—there's nothing going on down there."

"Again? How long has that been going on?" Charles asked.

"Couple of weeks, maybe longer. I've been catching up on my sleep," the security guard said.

No shit.

Charles shook his head in amazement and then filled in our names on the sign-in sheet. "I'm going to give these folks a tour. Lights and power on?"

"All the time, boss," the guard said. He opened a copy of the New York Post and began to read the sports section.

"What kind of staff do you have here today?" Charles asked.

"Just some folks in the control room up here. There's no one down in the pump station," the guard replied. I noticed the patch on the guard's jacket—it had an embroidered lighthouse with the name Beacon Security stitched above it. The city employed several independent companies to keep costs in check. My assumption was that Beacon was just one of the city's vendors.

Charles led us to a locker room. He looked at me. "Your jacket won't be warm enough." He handed us coats and protective helmets. "Put these on," he said. "It's cold and damp below. You won't like it very much."

Charles guided us to the elevator, and we descended into the pumping station. Charles wasn't kidding about not liking the environment. "Jesus, it's like the Himalayas down here." For a moment, I recalled how warm and toasty it was back at the precinct. *You're such a dope, Stephanie. Volunteering for work. That'll teach you.*

"I told you it wasn't pleasant," Charles said.

Gus zipped his jacket up to his neck. "Give us the ground rules," he said. "I'm too cold to stand still."

"Just watch your step," Charles said. "There's no telling where ice will form. And don't touch anything you think may be frozen. Your skin will instantly bond with the metal pipes. This station was built in the late sixties—safety standards were not as stringent back then as they are today. Use your heads."

There was no question that a body could be frozen down here. Judging by the upstairs guard's alert nature, I had no doubt that someone could slip a body in and out as well. The place was a ghost town because of the strike. Charles was a sharp guy, but my guess was that he didn't stop by very often.

The pumping station was astoundingly large. It had been blasted out of Manhattan bedrock, and the walls were pure stone. Water oozed from cracks in the bedrock in several locations. Some of the water was frozen. It was a little unnerving to think that the raging waters of the Hudson were just on the other side of the bedrock. The pipes running into the electric pumps were massive. "Might as well get cracking." As I said, the place was vast. I didn't know how much ground we could cover on our own. The size of the job warranted a full team of investigators. It was hard to fathom that places like this existed, but then I thought about how my last case led me to an old, forgotten railroad tunnel. There was another city beneath Manhattan, an entire network of tunnels and storerooms that time had long forgotten.

We spread out and began to look around. The pumping station was damp and brutally cold. I felt my teeth chattering as I searched for clues. I heard Gus shriek. I turned my head to see his legs fly out from beneath him. He was sitting on his butt, wincing in pain. I raced over to him, careful not to do the same. "You okay?" I called out. Gus was wearing his brave face and nodding so that I wouldn't worry. It was just about then that something crunched beneath my shoe. It wasn't a big clue, but it was obvious. It certainly wasn't something that belonged on the floor of a pumping station. I had crushed a small hypodermic syringe with my heel. It was on the ground near one of the mammoth water-delivery pipes. Gus was already up on his feet, so I knelt down to examine the syringe. As I did, something else caught my eye. A tuft of hair and a small section of skin were frozen to the huge, iron water pipe.

Chapter Eighteen

“**You** poor thing, you fell down and broke your butt.”

Gus bravely tried to smile through the pain, but I could see that he was really hurting as we walked back to our car. We left Charles at the pumping station, where he awaited the arrival of the crime scene investigators. “It’s embarrassing,” he said.

“What’s there to be embarrassed about? Do you really think that you’re first cop to fall on his keister in the line of duty? Just think about all of the sympathy sex I’m going to give you.” I became concerned when Gus didn’t reply to my comment. “I said sympathy sex—did you hear me?” Gus took a step and winced. “Do you want to see a doctor?”

“I’ll be all right. I just need a hot bath and a bottle of scotch.”

“How about a deep-tissue massage performed by yours truly?”

“It all sounds good. I just need to lie down for a while.”

I helped Gus into the car. I got into the driver’s seat and started the engine. “I’ll have you home in a jiffy. I’ll draw you a bath and get you doped up on Vicodin and whiskey. How’s that sound?”

“It sounds like a dream.” I watched as Gus squirmed in his seat and tried to get comfortable.

“Want me to whip out my boobs or something?”

“Now?”

“You look like you could use a distraction.”

Gus closed his eyes and put his head back against the headrest. "Not that I don't appreciate a good striptease every now and again, but how about you just drug me and put me to bed."

"Sure, no problem . . . Ingrate," I said, teasing him. "You know there are lots of guys that would get pretty excited over an offer like that."

"Baby, I'm dying here."

He wasn't responding to my charm, which meant that he was really in pain. I pressed the gas pedal and raced uptown. We were crossing 23rd Street when my cell phone rang. The caller ID read: Sonellio.

"Boss, is that you?"

Gus heard the excitement in my voice. It brought him around faster than a jolting whiff of smelling salts. "Nick's on the phone? Really? How is he?"

"Yes, yes, Stephanie, it's the old man. How are you?" Sonellio said.

"Happy, I'm so happy to hear your voice. Are you still up in Maine?"

"I'm home, Stephanie. I'm back in Staten Island."

"Really?" I didn't know whether his reply meant something good or bad. I'd been worried about his health for a long time now, and it overshadowed my exuberance. "Oh my God, we miss you so much. I'm here with Gus."

"Hi, boss," Gus shouted. He had so much adrenaline pumping through his veins that he had momentarily forgotten about his bruised butt. "We miss you, boss."

"I'm not the boss anymore," Sonellio said. "I'm just an old friend."

"You'll always be The Boss," Gus said aloud.

I smiled at Gus. Our feelings for Sonellio were so strong. Everything else felt unimportant in comparison. "So when are we going to see you?"

"Right away, if you can swing it. Any chance I can bribe the two of you into coming out for breakfast tomorrow?"

I whispered to Gus, "We don't have to be at the medical examiner's office until noon. We can run out to see him early in the morning. Okay?" Gus nodded happily. "Your place, boss?"

"Yeah. That okay?"

"I'd hijack the space shuttle if that's what it took." Sonellio laughed. It made me feel good to hear him chuckle, but then he coughed and a wave of melancholy washed over me. It was the same sickly cough I had heard from him increasingly just before he retired. "Eight o'clock good for you?"

"I'm up early," Sonellio said. "I'll put the coffee on, and it will be ready whenever you get here. I can't wait to see you, Stephanie. I miss you." There was sadness and finality in his last sentence. "Gus too."

"See you in the morning, boss. Give our love to Toni." I hung up and turned to Gus. I didn't know whether to smile or cry.

Chapter Nineteen

Toni Sonellio waved to us from the porch as we pulled up in front of her house. She pulled her sweater tight and hurried down the stairs to greet us. She threw her arms around me the moment I got out of the car.

"Oh my God, Stephanie, it's so good to see you." Toni took a step back to look me over. "You look great." She shrugged. "Where's the belly?"

My baby bump was beginning to look pretty obvious—Toni's comment was meant to flatter. I unbuttoned my jacket. *"Voila!"*

She ran her hand over my belly. "*Oh* . . . there it is. How far along are you?"

"Four and a half months."

"I can't believe how good you look. Did you put on any weight?"

"A ton," I said in an exaggerated manner.

"Well, you don't look it. Is the baby kicking yet?"

I shook my head. "I can't wait." I directed my next comment toward the baby. "Would you do something already—mommy's getting antsy."

Gus got out of the car from the passenger side. He was still sore from his slip-and-fall. He hobbled over to us and hugged Toni.

"What happened to you?" Toni asked.

"It's all the sex—I can't keep up with her," he said.

Toni rolled her eyes. "Yeah, go on. No seriously, what happened?"

"Gus fell down and broke his butt—it was job

related. How's the boss?"

Toni's head swayed back and forth. Her lips curled downward and her shoulders rose. "We're coming down the home stretch." She was quiet for a moment. "He'll be so happy to see you."

"What's been happening?" Gus asked.

Toni's eyes turned lifeless. "He's been fighting cancer for almost a year now, but . . . the treatments aren't helping anymore. We were up in Maine. He was fishing and I . . . okay, I was completely bored. All that fresh air seemed to be doing him good, and I was happy to knit and clean fish. You understand . . . but he's having trouble breathing, and the doctors don't know what else to do for him. We decided to come home, so that he could be around family and friends."

My throat tightened and then my arms were around Toni again. We both began to cry. "Get it out of your system before you go inside," she said. "The tears are tougher for him to swallow than the cancer."

I understood her completely. I had seen Sonellio deteriorate before my eyes, but he never complained and he never spoke about it. Sonellio had always been a rock. Men like him didn't respond to pity. Gus and I both knew what to expect—we had decided in advance to keep things upbeat. The grim reaper may have been close by, but there would be no talk of death today. Today, as always, Nick Sonellio was The Boss.

Toni and I dried our eyes. She inspected my face. "Waterproof makeup? You were always so smart." Gus looked like hell. The gravity of the situation was so intense that he seemed unable to lift his head. Toni lifted Gus' chin with her hand. "You're going to have to do better than that, Gus," Toni said. "Can you put on a happy face?" He nodded. It was sort of a hem-and-haw nod. I don't think he was convinced he could pull it off.

Gus wore his emotions on his sleeve. "Gus, are we good?" Toni asked with concern.

He took a deep breath. "I'm okay."

Toni put her arms around our waists and walked us into the house.

"Are they here?" I saw Sonellio at the top of the stairs. He smiled boldly and raced down the stairs in a manner which was meant to convey the impression that he was robust and healthy, but all the showmanship did not impress me. He looked like a sick man laboring to appear healthy. I tried, I really did, but a few tears escaped before I was able to sure up my armor.

"Tears? What's this?"

"I'm just so happy to see you."

"What the hell? I'm off the job six months and everyone falls apart? Pull yourself together, for God's sake." Sonellio gave me a kiss on the forehead just like my father used to. I don't know how I kept from going to pieces, but somehow I managed to hold myself together. Sonellio turned to Gus and noticed that he was limping as he walked toward him. "What the hell happened to you? You used to be a young buck."

"I took a bad fall," Gus said as he embraced Sonellio.

"Jesus, you look like hell, Gus. Isn't Stephanie taking care of you?"

"Trust me, she takes good care of me."

"Well then hell, let's eat breakfast." Sonellio clasped and wrung his hands. "I'm starving."

We began to walk toward the kitchen. I saw Toni prodding Sonellio with her elbow. "Oh yeah," Sonellio said. "Let me get a good look at you." I turned sideways so that the profile of my belly was noticeable. "You're pregnant? When did this happen . . . yesterday? You're as thin as a rail. Are you sure you're pregnant?"

"Yes, boss, I'm plenty pregnant."

"You'd better start eating. You want to give birth to a noodle or something?" Sonellio chuckled, and it brought some color to his cheeks. "Toni's been preparing all morning—we'll fatten you up."

We had picked up a small gift for the boss. I handed it to him in one of those fancy bags that everyone uses nowadays because we're all too busy or too lazy to use wrapping paper.

"The hell is this?" Sonellio protested.

"Just a little welcome-home present," Gus said.

"For Christ's sake, you gave me a watch for my retirement, the one without the numbers on it."

"The Movado?"

"Yeah, the Movado. I got it locked up in the safe deposit box."

"Why don't you use it?"

"A fancy watch like that? To go fishing?" He gave me a playful slap on the cheek. *"Sciocchezza."* It was the Italian word for silly. "What's in the bag, a polo mallet?"

"Something more practical," Gus said. "Take a look."

Sonellio reached into the bag and pulled out a bundled stack of DVDs. "*Star Trek*?"

"Every movie ever made," I said proudly.

"*Wrath of Kahn*?" Sonellio asked.

"It's in there," Gus said.

"He loves that movie," Toni said.

"I know. He used to walk around the precinct imitating Kahn, 'From hell's heart I stab at thee.'"

"How do you know I wasn't reciting *Moby Dick*?"

"*Moby Dick*? For real? You sounded just like Ricardo Montalban."

Sonellio cackled. "Christ, you really are a good detective. I'll put these to good use. Thanks. Goddamn it, let's eat!"

The house was filled with the aroma of sizzling

bacon. Toni had set the table with a pretty tablecloth and matching linen napkins.

"Bacon, eggs, *and* muffins? You really know how to treat a girl."

"Your mother would kick my ass if she heard that I didn't serve her daughter a good hot meal," Toni said. "Sit."

We took off our jackets and settled around the table. Gus was still squirming and trying to get comfortable. "You look like you've got ants in your pants, Gus," Sonellio said. "Have you seen a doctor?"

"No. I took a hot bath last night, and Stephanie got me loaded up on painkillers."

"You're walking like a duck," Sonellio said. "How about a shot of Sambuca?"

"At eight o'clock?"

"Sure, it'll take the edge off," Sonellio replied.

Gus was silent for a moment. It looked as if he were weighing his options. "Okay, what the hell," he replied. "The *pregmeister's* driving."

I was a little surprised that Sonellio had offered Gus a drink, and even more surprised that Gus accepted. Gus was obviously in a lot of pain. The fact that the offer had come from the boss made it okay. Sonellio was a highly moral person and a by-the-book cop. If he didn't have a problem with it . . .

Sonellio retrieved a bottle of Sambuca from the kitchen counter and poured a shot into Gus' juice glass. Sonellio partially covered his mouth and in an exaggerated loud voice said, "How long has he been twitching like this? If the hooch doesn't calm him down, I may have to shoot him."

Gus laughed and then winced. "What do you want from me? It hurts."

I stroked Gus' cheek. "You know what's good for

that?"

"What?"

"Kegels."

Toni laughed so hard that coffee sprayed out of her mouth. She recovered a moment later. "Same old Chalice," she said. She dished out the food, and we all got busy eating breakfast.

Gus winced as he reached for a biscuit on the other side of the table. I grabbed one for him and picked up a butter knife. "Easy there, big fella." I turned to Toni. "Men, they just love to butter the muffin." I winked at her, and she lost another ounce of coffee.

"Jesus, Stephanie, would you cut it out before I choke?" She turned to Gus. "You're a lucky man."

"I know," he said. "*Everyone* tells me. So, boss, how was the fishing?"

"Unbelievable, Gus. I caught bass the size of compact cars. You'd love it."

"He's not kidding," Toni said. She looked at me. "Stephanie, pray Gus doesn't become a fisherman. Do you have any idea what it's like to clean a twenty-pound fish? Do you know how stinky and smelly a job that is? Forget about getting the smell off your hands, *Madonna.* Pray, Stephanie, pray. Tell him you'll withhold sex—whatever it takes."

"So what's it going to be, Gus, bouillabaisse or me?" I gave him a smart-aleck grin.

"I can clean my own fish, thank you very much." Gus' expression said, *take that!*

Sonellio reached over and slapped Gus on the shoulder. "Atta boy," he said. "Show her you've got some stones." He laughed. "God I miss you guys."

We went into Sonellio's yard after breakfast. "Take a look over here," Sonellio said. "I want to show you something."

We followed him over to a storage shed in the corner of the yard. The two sliding doors had been sealed with paper-packaging tape, but the tape had been torn. It looked like it had been sprayed purple. Now, a layperson may not have known what that meant, but any cop worth his salt would pick up on that in a second. "You fingerprinted your shed?"

"I taped the doors before I left for Maine, knowing I'd be away for a while. I didn't want mice getting in and eating my lounge cushions.

"I don't know of any mice with fingerprints in the national database. Do you, Steph?" Gus chided.

"Smart ass," Sonellio barked. "Someone's been hanging around in my yard. I found torn denim on one of the fence caps and a pair of binoculars in the shed."

"Binoculars?"

Sonellio opened the shed. He handed me a large Ziploc bag with binoculars enclosed. He also handed me a small Ziploc containing a purple section of the tape, which had presumably been used to seal the shed doors. "Someone's been using my yard to spy on the neighbors. They obviously know that I've been away."

"So you want us to run the prints?" I asked.

"Would you, please? The whole thing is kind of creepy, and I don't want to bother the local police. I'm a former Chief of Detectives, for Christ's sake—I don't want to feel like I'm some kind of nuisance."

I looked at Gus and took the Ziplocs from Sonellio. I doubted that the local, second-story man had a set of prints in the IAFIS database, but humoring my old boss was the very least I could do. He had certainly done plenty for me. "No problem, boss."

"It's probably a local junkie looking to score some quick money for dope," Gus said.

"Could be," Sonellio replied. "But my house has been

empty for months, and no one has tried to get in."

"I can't believe you lifted the prints off the tape yourself. You still own a fingerprint kit?"

Sonellio laughed and then held his chest. My mind wandered to the small tank of oxygen I had seen sitting on the kitchen floor. "Not in thirty years. I bought a one-ounce bottle of gentian violet at Walmart for $2.99. I diluted it and used one of those travel-size spray bottles. I got some partials. I don't know if there's enough there for a match."

"You've still got it, boss," I said.

"And now you've got it, Stephanie. Find out who's been sneaking around my yard."

I raised my hand and spread my second and third fingers to form a Vulcan Salute. I didn't know how much time Sonellio had left, but I wanted to bestow my best wishes, "Live long and prosper."

Chapter Twenty

Anya Kozakova shuddered when she heard loud rapping on her apartment door, even though she was expecting a visitor. It sounded as if the door was being struck with a sledgehammer and would be knocked off the frame. She looked through the peephole and took a deep breath to steady her nerves. The courtyard window was exactly opposite her door, and the hallway was usually bright and well illuminated during daylight hours. Now, however, the massive individual standing outside her door prevented most of the sunlight from reaching the peephole.

"Tillerman?" she asked in her heavy Russian accent.

"Yes."

She opened the door. Michael Tillerman held up a thick, white envelope. "Can I come in?"

Kozakova nodded apprehensively and then stepped aside so that her massive visitor could enter. She closed the door behind him. She reached for the deadbolt, eyed her visitor once again, and then moved away from the door without engaging it. *Just in case,* she thought, *I may have to run.*

Tillerman handed her the envelope. "Here, count it," he said, "Two thousand dollars, all twenties."

She pointed to the kitchen table. "Have a seat," she said, trying to sound as strong and confident as possible. Her life in Soviet Georgia had not been easy. She had learned to project a stoic and impersonal demeanor in the face of a potential threat in order to appear fearless. It was a defense mechanism that had proven invaluable to her many times in the past. Tillerman took off his jacket and sat down. She sat down opposite him and began to count the cash. She made ten stacks of bills: two hundred dollars in each pile. She finished counting the money and stuffed it back into the envelope.

"Don't you want to put the money away?" Tillerman asked.

"What is the point?" Kozakova was a powerhouse but certainly no match for Tillerman. "You could snap my neck in two seconds. "*Медведь (med-ved'),*" she mumbled.

"What does that mean?"

"It's Russian for bear. You look like some kind of huge creature."

Tillerman had come directly from the gym. His hair was wild and his muscles were still pumped. His shoulders and arms extended out of his athletic shirt like broad tree limbs. "Don't worry," Tillerman said. "I don't want to kill you."

"Good, I don't want to die. Did you bring your electronic ID tag?"

"Da." Tillerman's lips and chin twisted in opposite directions, forming an odd smile.

"That's funny," Kozakova said. "Now you're a funny bear."

Tillerman reached into his pants pocket and withdrew his electronic security tag. He placed it on the table.

Kozakova took the tag over to her workstation. She was a brilliant programming engineer. She had assembled an array of modified computers and processing devices, which she had cannibalized from bits and parts that had been discarded by high-end gamers and computer geeks. She had learned to program in C++ and Python before she turned twelve.

"You've got a lot of equipment over there," Tillerman said. "What is all of that?"

Kozakova turned back and saw that Tillerman was examining her equipment with interest. "You're an engineer?" she asked.

"No."

"Then there is no point in trying to explain. You wouldn't understand." She entered several commands on the keyboard. After a moment, the LEDs on a small device began to flash. She swiped Tillerman's security tag through it and then stood up. "Here," she said as she handed the tag back to Tillerman. "You can go."

"That's it?" Tillerman asked with surprise in his voice.

"That's it. You'll have access to all of Vicor's restricted areas—all of the programming was completed before you arrived. You think you paid two thousand dollars for nothing? I put in five hours of programming time on your silly little security tag."

He looked at the tag in his immense hand before he slipped it back into his pocket. "I see. I am glad that you took your assignment seriously."

"Don't worry," she said. "I know better than to poke the bear."

Chapter Twenty-one

“**Goodness**, it’s the baby *madda.*” Glenaster Tully sprung from his desk chair the moment Gus and I walked into the medical examiner’s office. Tully was Jamaican and spoke with a heavy accent. He was beaming with exuberance as we embraced. “*Cha-lee-see,* you look like a blossoming orchid.”

Really, a blossoming orchid? Oh well, maybe it was one of his Jamaican things. It sounded like a sweet analogy, at any rate.

Tully turned to Gus and gave him a playful elbow in the side. “Nice work, baby papa. You two are going to have a beautiful child.” Tully was the kind of guy you just had to like. He was happier than a family of chipmunks—cartoon chipmunks, anyway. “How are you feeling?”

“I’m great, my friend—happy, healthy, and ready to kick some ass.”

“You ain’t slowed down yet?” Tully asked.

“Nah. I just carry a supply of barf bags with me at all times. Otherwise, I’m good to go. How about you?”

“Fabulous, *mon,* really fabulous. My kids are coming to live with me. They’ll be here next month.”

Somewhere in the back of my mind, I remembered that Tully had a family in Jamaica, but he rarely spoke about them. I tried not to appear surprised. “That’s great. What about your wife?”

Tully’s smile disappeared for a moment. “Nah, *mon,* that’s a fuckery. She done picked up with another *mon*—

don't want the kids neither."

"Fuckery?" Gus asked.

"Yeah, *mon*, she's messed up," Tully said. "She's not doing right by the kids."

"I'm sorry to hear that. How old are they?"

"Eight and ten—I ain't seen them in two years. My heart's breaking, *Cha-lee-see*." He looked at the floor, and when he looked up all traces of unhappiness were gone. "I just rented a bigger place. Can't wait for them to get here." He pulled out his wallet and showed us a picture of his children.

"Cute kids!" Gus said.

"They look like their father. I'm really happy for you." I gave Tully a second hug. "Oh, hey, can you check these for prints?" I handed Tully an evidence bag, which contained the binoculars and tape sample that Sonellio had given us. I didn't want to bring up Sonellio's name—he was a very private man. "It may have to do with our investigation."

"That's easy," Tully said as he took the bag from me. "No problem."

"So, do you have any test results on John Doe yet?"

"Just starting to come through now. I'll tell you what I know."

We followed Tully over to an examination table. Plastic evidence bags containing the hair and scalp samples that had been frozen to the pump station water pipe were lying on the table.

"What do you think?" Gus asked.

"The hair looks like a match to the John Doe that was found in Kowsky Plaza—same texture and color. We won't know for sure until we have a DNA workup, and that will be late tomorrow. I looked for the section of scalp that had been ripped from Doe's head when it was frozen to the pipe, but the area is too small and the hair follicles are too dense. I didn't find anything."

"What was in the crushed syringe?"

"Special K."

"Ketamine. I'm not surprised." Ketamine is a very strong tranquilizer which is commonly abused on the street. "He likely died of hypothermia while under sedation and froze due to his close proximity to the Hudson water inlet."

"Hey!" Tully protested good-humoredly. "Who's the expert around here?"

"Oops. Sorry. So what do you think?"

"I think you know your shit, *Cha-lee-see*. Maybe you can cover for me when I go on vacation with my kids."

"No way, Tully. I belong out on the street, just me, Gus, and the barf bags."

"How far along are you? The nausea should be subsiding," Tully said.

"Yeah, it's getting better. I'm past the halfway point."

"Is the baby kicking yet?"

"Only when I eat burritos."

Tully laughed. "That ain't the baby kicking. That's your mama gas."

Where is this conversation going? First I'm a blossoming orchid and now I've got mama gas. Time to move on. "How about the autopsy?"

"Did you find Special K in the tox screen?" Gus asked.

"Ain't back yet. Everything is slow on account that we had to defrost the body—maybe later today, but I would say it's likely because John Doe didn't take off his clothes."

"You'll have to explain that one to me."

"When body temperature drops too much, the heart rate becomes slow and weak, and the blood vessels widen. It makes the victim feel hot and confused," Tully said. "They want to remove all their clothes before they finally slip into unconsciousness. Then the heart stops. There are lots of stories about mountain climbers found naked and dead on a mountain with their clothes lying nearby. There was no evidence that John Doe was bound. I think John Doe didn't take off his clothes because he was unconscious."

"That's a drag," Gus said.

"At least he wasn't' feeling any pain. I know we're testing for specific Y-STR markers and haplogroups, but those reports aren't back yet—even with current technology, we need a full eight hours. I'll let you know when they're in." Tully checked his watch. "You nice folks clocking out after this?" He reached into the pocket of his lab coat and gave us a quick peek at his one-hitter pipe. He checked to make sure that he wouldn't be overheard. "I've got some great shit."

Gus seemed shocked. "Jesus, you've got pot?"

Yes, Gus, he's got pot. He's been smoking as long as we've known him. I think the painkillers had knocked Gus for a loop.

"Where'd you get it?" Gus asked.

He scored it on the black market. He bartered for it with nylon stockings and Hershey Bars. Jesus, Gus, what kind of question is that?

"I got me some good friends," Tully said with a sly smile. "What y'all say?"

"Not for me. Thanks."

"Ah, *Cha-lee-see*, it can't hurt you."

"I gave up wine. Do you think I'm going to smoke pot?"

"I could use a hit," Gus said.

My eyes must have popped out like I was Roger Rabbit. *"What?"*

"Have some sympathy. My back is killing me," Gus

said. His comment shed light on the silly questions he had asked Tully. I guess it was Gus' way of testing the waters. "I just had a random drug test—I doubt I'll be asked for a urine sample any time soon."

"I thought you were standing kind of funny," Tully said. "This shit will fix you right up."

I gave Tully a kiss on the cheek. "Fine, you heal the baby papa. I'll wait in the car."

Chapter Twenty-two

Brian Spano wiped his mouth with a paper napkin and screwed the cap back onto his empty bottle of water. He checked the time. He had five minutes left on his dinner break and was determined to enjoy every minute of it. He still had a few minutes to rest before going back on the clock. He shook the crumbs from the plastic bag in which his tuna fish sandwich had been packed and pressed it flat with his hands before replacing it in his blue and white Igloo lunchbox. The lunchbox bore the name: Little Playmate. It was the lunchbox his seven-year-old son considered dorky and would no longer take with him to school. It was hardly a man's lunchbox, but Brian wasn't throwing anything away these days. Lunchboxes, plastic bags, Poland Spring water bottles; he used and recycled everything until they were completely shot. Divorce had taken everything from him, all except for his son Alex, whom he saw every other weekend.

When did everything get so bad? He had three minutes left to revel in the solitude of *leave me the hell alone*. He had three precious minutes left to purge his mind and forget about child-support payments and threatening letters from his wife's attorney.

Good thing that I'm so small, he mused. *It doesn't take much to fill me up.*

They were just kids when he and his wife first met on summer break after high school graduation. He was naïve and she was clueless. They were both lonely. She became pregnant with Alex before the fall. *The fall,* he thought. It was a metaphor for his life.

His electronic Timex watch beeped. He stood as if by cue and walked to the door of the employee cafeteria. The sign on the wall read: Vicor Pharmaceuticals, Employee Suite. A packet of salt had been left behind on one of the lunch tables. He put it in his pocket. *Nothing goes to waste.*

He had been checking the inventory of the clinical test medications once per week, but the company's compliance department now felt the routine insufficient. He was now required to check the inventory twice each week. It was an extra two hours work, which had to be completed within the confines of his regular shift. "Good going, compliance department," he said aloud.

It was 9:30 p.m. The building was usually dead silent at that hour, but Spano heard noises coming from within the storeroom as he approached. He swiped his security pass to enter the room. He immediately saw torn cartons of drugs on the floor. A towering shadow rose over him. He had to crane his neck in order to see the face of the behemoth that stood before him.

"Hey! What the hell are you doing in here?" Spano said. "You're not supposed to—" A huge hand grabbed him by the throat and choked off his words. He tried to grab his attacker's arm, but it was too thick for him to get his hands around. He couldn't breathe. In the next instant, he was suspended in the air, his eyes level with the wires that had been torn from the ceiling security camera. He felt lightheaded. His son's face flashed before his eyes, and then he heard a snap. His world went black.

Chapter Twenty-three

"**How** do you feel?"

I had been watching Gus sleep for the past few minutes. Frankly, I was admiring him and thinking about how his strong jaw and thick, brown hair might translate if we had a little boy. I watched as he opened his eyes to greet the morning. He stretched in response to my query, testing his injured back.

"I think it's a little better."

I stroked his hair. "I guess Tully's weed did you some good."

"It definitely helped me relax." A hint of embarrassment was present in Gus' response. He obviously felt guilty about toking with Tully. He must have been in great discomfort to do something like that, even though it was at the end of our shift. I wasn't going to take him to task over it. I gave him a mental *get out of jail free* card. I hated the idea of him filling his lungs with smoke—especially now with the boss succumbing to the ravages of lung cancer. *One free pass, mister, that's all you get.*

I snuggled next to Gus. I heard him sigh, and then his breathing became heavy. Before I knew it, he had fallen back to sleep. I peered over his shoulder and out the window. I wasn't quite ready to get out of bed, but my mind was already back on the clock. I began to think about our visit with Tully and the meager amount of new information we had learned from him. We learned that John Doe had been drugged with ketamine—or Special

K, as it was known on the street. Special K had become a pretty popular street drug, particularly at dance clubs and raves. It had psychoactive properties and could alter mood and behavior. At low doses, it produced a mild, dreamy feeling, as well as a feeling of being slightly outside one's body. Higher doses produced a hallucinogenic effect. *And to think, they use it on horses. Some people will try anything.* We were still waiting for John Doe's DNA report, so we had no idea if he was in any way related to victim number one. I didn't feel like the whiz-bang detective everyone needed me to be, nor did I feel like the detective I wanted to be. I wondered if the childbearing process had altered my thought processes. Was I less clever than I used to be? There was a pair of murders to be solved and I didn't feel as if I had made any progress. One of the maternity books I read referenced something called pregnancy brain. *Maybe that's what's going on.*

The phone rang and startled Gus. "Five more minutes," he pleaded.

"Shhh." I grabbed the phone and pulled the bedroom door closed behind me. I went into the kitchen so that Gus could get a few more minutes rest. "Hold on," I said into the phone.

"Stephanie, it's me, Nick." Sonellio's voice was filled with panic and anger.

"Boss? What wrong?"

"Did you run those prints yet?" He wasn't asking nicely. He was upset, and his tone was urgent.

"I dropped them off right after we had breakfast with you. Why, has something happened?"

"Turn on the news. A family was murdered last night." I worked for Nick Sonellio for years, and as hard as it is for me to say, we had both heard this kind of news before. We worked homicide. Death was our business. Death is what pays our bills. In all that time, I had never heard Sonellio sound so dire. I had never heard such utter devastation in his voice.

"Boss, what's wrong?"

"I told you! I told you something was wrong." Sonellio began to cough into the phone. His cough grew significantly louder. It sounded as if he couldn't control it.

"Boss, settle down. Talk to me."

Toni's voice came on the line. "Just a minute." I heard a hiss. "Easy, Nick, easy. Breathe," I heard her say. She was silent for a moment. I strained my ears and listened carefully to the sound of Sonellio's labored breathing. I had spent enough time in hospitals to know what I was hearing. He was inhaling oxygen. It took a couple of moments, but his coughing eventually subsided. I turned on the TV and flipped to the local news station. A news reporter was interviewing neighbors. The information banner at the bottom of the screen read: Staten Island Family Slain.

"Stephanie?" Toni was back on the line. "Can he call you back? He—" I could hear Toni sobbing.

"Toni, what's wrong? Tell me what's going on." The news camera pulled back, providing a wide-angle view of the street. I was able to read the corner street signs: Bancroft Avenue and Edison Street. It took a second, but then I understood why Sonellio was in such distress. The family that had been slain lived around the corner from him. They were his neighbors.

Chapter Twenty-four

I felt an ache in my chest as we retraced the very same route we had taken to Sonellio's house just the other day. Gus was feeling better and was behind the wheel as we crossed over the Verrazano Bridge to Staten Island. I was preoccupied with the thought of Sonellio's dead neighbors and was glad that Gus was driving. Sonellio was a righteous man. I couldn't imagine how hard the news had hit him. He had most likely been accurate—someone had used his yard to case his neighbors' homes. He was so close. Close enough to prevent what happened? Never! But Nick Sonellio was not the kind of guy to let himself off the hook. *He must be devastated.*

We were on our way to pick up Sonellio. A courtesy call had been made to the Staten Island assistant chief of detectives, who was a longtime friend of Sonellio's. He graciously extended investigative privileges to the three of us.

I felt myself growing more and more tense as we got closer. I had the same directions in my hand as the other day and was reading out the turns: Richmond Road, Bancroft Avenue, and then finally Clawson Street. Toni was sitting on the front steps, blotting her eyes with a tissue. She looked up and I could see that her eyes were bright red. I had the door open before the car came to a stop. I ran to her. She stood, and I threw my arms around her. "Toni, I'm so sorry."

She began to cry. "Jesus, Stephanie, my girls used to

babysit for them."

Gus joined us a second later. It was a truly terrible moment.

The front door opened, and Sonellio stepped out. He was dressed in a dark suit. His expression scared me—I could see the enormous strain on his face. The timing was terrible—it seemed as if whatever time he had left had been cut in half by this new emotional nightmare. It was a hell of an ordeal for a mortally-ill man to face.

Sonellio tugged on his tie to straighten it and then approached us. Toni looked at him with tears in her eyes and kissed him on the cheek. She recognized the look on her husband's face: all business. It was time for her to step aside and let him do his job.

"It's cold out here," Sonellio said to her. "Go inside. I'll call you when I'm on my way home."

"You don't have to call," she said. "It's only around the—" Toni started to shake. She gazed at us with a horrified expression on her face and then quickly ran into the house.

Sonellio barely looked at us as he got into the car. The car doors slammed. The interior compartment was completely silent, silent in an unnerving way.

"Did you bring the evidence?" Sonellio asked.

"Yes," I replied. Sonellio's find had not yielded any meaningful results. The binoculars did not bare any fingerprints, and the prints on the tape were only partials that the lab was unable to match through IAFIS, the FBI-maintained Integrated Automated Fingerprint Identification System. "I'll take them, thanks," he said and held out his hand. I handed the evidence bags back to him. "I thought I was one step ahead of this bastard," he continued "I wasn't. We *will* find him." There was no question as to his resolve. "This SOB killed my neighbor, his wife, and their two boys. I know that I have no right to ask for your help on this case, but I'm going to ask anyway."

"It's all right, boss," Gus said. "You don't have to ask—whatever you need, you've got. We're here for you." I'm sure Sonellio assumed that we were working on other cases. It didn't seem to matter to him.

Sonellio reached over and patted Gus on the cheek. He rested his hand on my shoulder. I looked back—in that glance, he shared with me his most private thought. It was as if he was saying, *one last time, okay?* I nodded and turned away before I lost control. I just couldn't deal with the implication—it was his way of saying goodbye.

When we arrived at the crime scene, Sonellio surrendered the evidence bags to a crime scene investigator and related the circumstances under which the items had been discovered, ensuring that the chain of evidence had not been broken. Richard Forzo, the Staten Island assistant chief of detectives, arrived shortly afterward. He called out to the boss from the doorway. "Chief Sonellio." They embraced for a long moment. Sonellio had known Forzo for years. He had appointed Forzo to the assistant chief's position. "I'm so sorry, Nick. We'll catch this son of a bitch. I promise you." He took a step back. I saw that he was giving Sonellio a quick once over. It didn't take much of an investigative mind to evaluate his current state of health. I saw Forzo's expression become concerned. In the next second, he switched gears. "Everyone, a moment," he called out to the NYPD staff on site. "This is my former boss, Chief of Detectives Nick Sonellio. He is assisting the department with this investigation, and you will extend him *every* courtesy. Am I understood?" The investigators all confirmed with nods. He pointed to Gus and me. "These two detectives are assisting Chief Sonellio, and you will treat them with the same level of courtesy."

Forzo continued to instruct his staff, but I was already thinking about the crime scene. His voice faded into the background as I began to look around the house. Pictures of the family were displayed on the wall that led to the upper level of the home. The Jacobys had been a handsome family; now they were murder victims. A crystal vase on a side table near the stairs was filled with white lilies. The proximity of the flowers to the family pictures seemed so sad and final to me. *What kind of person murders an entire family?*

"I guess we never know what life has in store for us." Forzo was standing behind me. "A beautiful family like this . . . so much to live for." He extended his hand and waited for me to accept. "You're Detective Chalice, right?"

"Call me Stephanie."

"I knew your dad. He was a good man. I learned a lot from your father and Nick." He shook his head. "What's going on with my old friend? He doesn't look very good."

My head dropped. "He's got lung cancer."

"Oh Jesus." Forzo covered his mouth for a moment. "That's not fucking fair. Nick worked like a dog his whole life and now this? I don't think he's retired a year yet."

"Just over six months."

"Terrible. The people who say police pensions are too rich should know what this job takes from us: our health, our sanity, and our futures. I know how close the two of you are. Nick talks about you like you're one of his kids."

My throat started to tighten. "Don't do this to me now. I won't be able to focus on the case."

"Sorry." Forzo reached into his pocket and handed me his business card. "Call me," he said. "Anytime, day or night. Nick is that important to me. Good luck,

Detective. Help us catch this monster. Let's do it for the boss." He turned and walked away.

The killer must have surprised Sherri and Bruce Jacoby in the kitchen. He was efficient and precise. They had both been shot through the heart, taken down with just one bullet each. The two boys had been shot in an upstairs bedroom. They were both wearing headphones and playing video games. I doubt they heard their parents being murdered or the assailant's footsteps as he crept up behind them and took their lives too. As with the parents, he had killed each boy with one fatal bullet.

"He knew the exact location of the heart," the blood spatter expert said. "Just left of center—the shooter has a working knowledge of the human anatomy. A lot of people think they know where the heart is located, but they don't. Especially when he shot the boys upstairs. It's hard to approximate the position of the heart from a dorsal view of the target."

"What kind of animal does something like this?" I asked him.

"I don't know. I don't see many like this; you?"

"An entire family? No. What motive could someone possibly have for causing this much pain?"

"You'd know better than me, Detective. I just determine how the killer did it. These kids and their folks were all shot at extremely close range."

"He shot the kids in the back while they were playing video games. They had both been wearing headphones. The first responder said that when he removed the headphones from the boys, the volume was deafening—they never heard him coming."

I thought about my baby. Life is so precious. *How could anyone . . .* "I don't think I'll ever understand this level of mental illness, no matter how hard I try." But I knew someone who might. “Excuse me,” I said and walked just outside the front door to where it was a little quieter. I took out my cell phone and called Nigel Twain.

Chapter Twenty-five

I met Nigel at Josie's West on Amsterdam at 74th. Honestly, the prospect of eating at a restaurant known for its veggie and vegan specialties didn't exactly turn me on. I had a craving for eggplant parm and garlic knots—tofu and kale was just not going to cut it. Fortunately, I discovered that they served lots of other great stuff. I had a warm, macadamia-crusted, chicken breast salad and was already drooling over the prospect of devouring a chocolate chip cookie dough ice cream pie for dessert.

Nigel Twain was a dear friend, an inspired thinker, and psychiatrist who had helped with cases before. He was what you might call an unconventional soul. I valued his thoughts on the human mind and hoped that he could better help me understand the warped individual who had stolen the futures from the members of the Jacoby family.

"This salad is absolutely scrumptious." I still had food in my mouth as I spoke. "I have to say that I was really surprised when you picked this place."

Twain was a gorgeous, dark, and complicated man with a sexy English accent. I always found his voice stimulating. Now, however, with the workings of my body all atwitter, my response to the sound of his voice was even stronger. You can blame it on the hormones if you want to, but for some reason every one of my erogenous zones seemed to resonate in sync to his deep baritone vibrato. I have had to practice extreme self-control from the very first day I met Nigel, and it wasn't getting any easier. I was doing my best to ignore his manly good looks—staring down at my salad instead of making contact with his piercing eyes—but his voice . . . I mean what could I do? I couldn't stick my fingers in my ears. There was no way to block it out.

"I've given up absolutely everything that's bad for me," Twain replied. "I was getting too indulgent." He patted his stomach, which by the way was as flat as a washboard. "I'm getting to that age where I have to pay more attention to what I put in my mouth."

"No pot?"

"Not a puff."

"No absinthe?'

"Not a sip."

"Sounds pretty boring."

"Oh, it's bloody tedious and going to the gym is even worse. I much prefer imbibing, indulging, and carrying on."

"You left out cavorting."

"That word does not deserve a place in an English gentleman's vocabulary."

"English gentleman, really? Is that how you see yourself?" Twain smirked. "You look like you're holding up pretty well." Twain had been a wild one, all right—he had experimented with LSD in his younger days as a method to better understand the human psyche. He was obsessive-compulsive when I first met him—and germophobic to the nth degree. He's much better these days, but who really knew what was going on in his head. I'd learned to look past all that. Twain was a sincere and loyal friend with a mind equaled by few. Oh by the way, the scent of his truffle-infused mashed potatoes was driving me out of my mind. "Can I steal some of those?"

Twain looked down at his plate. "The beef or the potatoes?"

"The potatoes. The aroma is driving me wild."

Twain was generous to a fault. He hesitated, and I immediately understood why—he wouldn't be able to go near his food once I had touched it with my fork. I guess a few of those germy little bugs were still scurrying around inside his head. I grabbed a sparkling clean fork from the next table. "Spotless—can I? Just one bite. I promise." Twain gestured to his plate. Those heavenly potatoes were in my mouth and caressing my taste buds within seconds. "Oh my God, those are incredible."

Twain plopped a pile on my dish. "Never let it be said that Nigel Twain deprived an expectant mother. Better, *mum*?"

"Much. You're a real friend." I was scoffing down his potatoes along with my macadamia-encrusted chicken. It was so good, I think in some ways it qualified as a religious experience.

"A pity that Gus couldn't tag along. I haven't seen him in ages," Twain said.

I couldn't tell Twain about this, but Gus was a little jealous of him. Gus once caught me talking about Twain in my sleep while in the midst of a hot and steamy fantasy. It caused hurt feelings, and to this day, Gus still looks at Twain as an opponent. Nothing has ever happened between the two of us, but I'd be lying if I didn't admit that I found him incredibly desirable. Twain was the flickering flame, and I had to be extra careful not to dance too close to the fire. "He's reviewing the crime scene findings back at the station house . . . while I probe you about the psychological aspects of the case." *Probe, now that was a word I could have easily left out of our conversation—practice better self-control, girl.* "Do you want to look at the crime scene photos now, or do you want to wait until after we've finished eating? They're pretty bad."

"I didn't think you asked me here to look at Disney World snapshots. Let's have at 'em."

I pulled a folder out of my bag and slid it across the table. Twain cut a piece of steak and examined the photos while he ate. I watched his expression. He didn't seem overly distressed. I didn't break stride either—I was still munching away on the heavenly combination of chicken and mashed potatoes.

"May I ask the caliber of the bullet that was used?"

"9mm."

"Anything special about the slug?"

"Special?" Twain knew little about bullets and guns, so I was surprised by the question. "There's only limited information back from the lab—what are you looking for?"

"Just the basics."

"I see. The slugs are hollow points, soft metal, unjacketed."

"That's what I was looking for."

"Really? When did you become a ballistics expert?"

"Only one of the victims had an exit wound—follow?"

I understood immediately. I smiled at Twain to acknowledge the fact that he had impressed me. Bullets made of soft metal and bullets that are unjacketed tend to flatten out upon impact. They transfer their energy more efficiently than hard metal, jacketed bullets, which are more likely to keep on going until they exit the body. Whoever killed the Jacoby family had committed four murders and used only four bullets in the process. "So you believe that the killer specifically chose hollow points, knowing that they do the most internal damage?"

"There's more to it than that, love—small entrance wound, less chance of an exit wound, and all the damage occurs inside the body."

"Meaning?"

"He didn't want the bodies mutilated. He wanted them to appear pristine in death. He wanted them to appear serene and peaceful."

"Why?"

"Any number of possible reasons, but right now I'll have to go with *I don't know.*"

"You don't know?"

"No."

"But you've got a hunch, don't you?"

"Most certainly." Twain finished chewing his bite of food and then met my gaze straight on. "You take good care of the things you want to keep. My guess is that these victims are the assailant's trophies. Whoever did this wants to retain the image of this family as they were in life and didn't want that image tarnished with a lot of blood and exposed flesh."

"Do you think he took pictures of them?"

"He may have indeed. Then again I'm not sure. The diseased mind doesn't work like yours or mine. The image of this family may already be burned into his memory."

Chapter Twenty-six

Brian Spano awoke in a large field. The morning sun had just begun to rise. The first few rays burned his eyes as he squinted to see where he was. It took a second for him to settle in. "Oh thank God," he said aloud. "I'm alive." He scanned the large field and saw that he was alone. He began to breathe nervously as one thought linked to the next and to the next. A face filled his mind and terrorized him. He began to breathe frantically. It was the giant's face. The face of a man so large and frightening that it caused him to tremble. *But I'm alive,* he told himself. *Take it easy, Brian. You'll be all right.* His rapid breathing began to slow down. He tested his legs and then stood. As he did, a terrible pain shot through his neck and restored the memory of a huge hand encircling his throat and a mammoth arm lifting him into the air. He rubbed his neck to soothe the pain, but it did not help.

Where the hell am I? Brian looked around and saw that the field was littered with trash. The air smelled with a putrid odor. He felt something sting him and saw that red fire ants were swarming on one of his shoes and crawling up his leg. "Shit." He brushed them off as best he could but the ants continued to bite him all the while. *This is the least of my problems.*

Something moved in the brush nearby that startled him. It didn't take long for him to see that a rat was gnawing on a discarded box of crackers. He walked in the opposite direction, brushing the ants from his leg every few steps. He heard a noise that he had recently learned to detest. It was the sound a sanitation truck makes when its hydraulic winch engages to lift the trash dumpster. The bedroom of his new apartment was on a busy street, and the sanitation trucks woke him prematurely two to three days a week. *Jesus, I'm in a goddamn garbage dump.* The sanitation truck was a quarter mile off in the distance, and the path to it was blocked with refuse and vermin. He took a deep breath and hurried toward salvation.

~~~

Spano was strapped to a gurney. He was wearing a neck brace, and an IV line had been inserted into his arm. He was staring up at the roof of the ambulance when a uniformed cop got into the ambulance and sat down next to him.

"How are you doing, buddy?" the cop asked.

Spano spoke in a hoarse voice. "Okay, I suppose."

"I'm Officer Nowicki, Stan Nowicki. The EMS guys said someone dumped you here at the kills. Jesus, what the hell happened?" Nowicki took out a pad and began to make notes.

"I'm an inventory clerk at Vicor Pharmaceuticals."

"Oh yeah," Nowicki said. "I've seen that place, over by the Outer Bridge Crossing. They tell me your name is Brian. Is that right?"

"Brian Spano."

"So how'd you get here, Brian?"

"I don't know." Spano sighed. He tried to move, but he was strapped down securely. "I'd just finished my dinner break. I was about to go back on duty when I heard noises coming from the storeroom. Next thing I know, some giant monkey has me by the throat and—"

"And?"
~~~

"The guy was a monster. He lifted me up in the air. I started to black out, and then I woke up in the dump."

"Do you remember what he looked like?"

"That's all I remember, that big fucking head of his. Shit, I thought I was gonna die."

"Well you're still here, Brian. The emergency service guys are taking good care of you. I'll be out of your hair in a minute, and they'll take you over to the hospital to get checked out."

"Which one?"

"Which hospital? Staten Island University Hospital. Good place. They'll check out your neck and make sure it's not broken." Nowicki saw his partner walking by outside the ambulance. "Hey, Ray, can you get on the horn? Find out if a break-in was reported over at Vicor, okay?

"Got it," Ray said.

"You'll have to give us a full statement, but a detective can get that from you in the hospital. Anyone you want us to notify?"

A lump formed in Spano's throat while he thought about his ex-wife and whether she would care that he had been attacked. "I just got divorced."

"Oh, sorry to hear that. Look, I'm sure she'll want to know. Got any kids?"

"Yeah, my son Alex."

Nowicki smiled. "Your son will tie the two of you together forever. Trust me, *I know*."

Chapter Twenty-seven

Tillerman hoisted the body of the mammoth Russian onto his shoulder, closed the doors of his panel van, and trudged back to the funeral parlor. The Russian was heavy on his shoulders, not because of the weight but because the body continued to shift back and forth as he walked down the steps to the basement crematorium. Tillerman routinely cleaned and jerked more than four hundred pounds, and the Russian by his estimation was scarcely over three hundred.

He missed a step on the way down. His legged slipped out from under him, and he felt a hard pop in his left thigh. The pain was severe and far worse than any physical pain he had ever felt before. He regained his footing but not before the Russian's head smacked into the staircase wall. "Ah shit!" Pain coursed up his leg and into his gut. He stopped momentarily to compose himself. He pressed the Russian between his shoulder and the brick staircase wall. His right hand was now free, and he used it to rub his face and calm himself while he fought off the overwhelming desire to vomit. He waited a moment and hoped that the pain would subside, but it didn't, and the weight of the Russian did not help. He could feel his injured leg begin to cramp as the huge muscles attempted to lock in spasm. *Move! Move*. He attempted to step down with his uninjured leg, but the left leg buckled, and he went down. The Russian hit the stairs with a thud and rolled down to the basement floor. He cursed himself. The abductor group of muscles was one of the few muscle groups he ignored—most men did. It was for sissies. The exercise for the abductors was performed on a "ladies machine," a machine that women used to tone and slim their thighs.

He sat down on the steps, rested with his head in his hands, and gazed between his open fingers at the body sprawled out on the stone floor in front of him. It felt like the muscle tear went all the way down to the bone. Pain seared his leg—it was as if a red-hot branding iron was pressed against his inner thigh.

"Fire, fire, fire, fire," he began to chant, a loud guttural chant. *Think past the pain!* "Fire, fire, fire." He clenched his fist and continued to chant "fire," making it a mantra to see him through the pain and allow him to continue on his quest. "Fire!" Tillerman exploded off the steps, hopping on his one strong leg until he had reached the body. He knelt down alongside the Russian and used his immense upper-body strength to lift him and roll him back onto his shoulder. He stood and balanced in a way as to not put any pressure on his damaged leg. He began a series of short hops—one excruciating thrust after another. Moments later, he slammed the body into a cremation container, much in the same way he would cast away a heavy barbell after completing a set of heavy lifts.

Tillerman was completely spent and laid on top of the open cremation container for a moment. He reached into his back pocket and fished out the Russian's wallet. The name on the drivers' license read Marat Vetrov. The picture on the drivers' license was dark and shadowy. It made Vetrov appear even more menacing than he actually was. Vetrov was a huge man, taller than Tillerman and heavier. He did not have Tillerman's body-builder physique, but he was massive in every respect. It would normally have taken three men to bring him down, but Tillerman caught him off guard and snapped his neck with one violent twist. He compared the drivers' license photo to the face of the man lying in the cremation box. *A big hairy bear*, Tillerman mused, *a monstrous grizzly bear.* A word formed on his lips. It was a word he had heard only once, but it had stuck with him and rolled smoothly off his tongue: "*Медведь* (med-ved)." It was the word the Russian woman had used to describe Tillerman, but the description better suited Vetrov. "So that's how you got into Vicor." Tillerman said aloud. "That's how you came to steal my pills." He brought the image of Anya Kozakova to mind. He had not been with a woman since his wife's murder, but Anya's contours roused him. She was formidable and strong in appearance with large pillows for breasts and a thin, cruel mouth that intrigued him. He thought he had seen her for the last time, but he now knew that he would have to see her again, if for no other reason but to complete the ritual. Vetrov was number three. He needed just one more. "She betrayed me. Why? For more money? What does she need with my pills?" He closed the wallet and tossed it haphazardly into the cremation box.

Vetrov's eyes were wide open. He screamed when Tillerman pulled the duct tape off his mouth. Blood trickled from the corner of his mouth. His eyes were filled with terror as he looked up at Tillerman. "Why?" he said in a trembling voice. Blood gurgled in his throat from the socket Tillerman had made removing his teeth—he struggled not to choke. Tillerman had snapped his neck, but the trauma had not proven fatal—Vetrov was paralyzed from the shoulders down.

Tillerman said nothing and lined up the cremation box up with the opening of the furnace. Vetrov angled his glance and saw the furnace in front of him. His lips began to quiver, and tears ran down from the corners of his eyes. "Why?" he repeated as he tried to make sense of what was going on. "Don't do this!"

Tillerman picked up the lid of the cremation container and held it over Vetrov. He looked down at the paralyzed giant and then closed his eyes. "Blessed are the elements of life. May the fire consume you."

He reignited his chant. "Fire, fire, fire!" He grew louder and louder, summoning his innermost reserves. He slammed the lid down on top of the box and sealed it. He set the controls and then pushed the cremation box into the furnace. "Death by fire!" he roared as the flames leapt up inside the furnace and consumed his sacrifice.

Chapter Twenty-eight

Nick Sonellio pushed on the glass door to enter Café Baci. It was early morning, hours before the café opened for lunch. The restaurant was so quiet that he would have been able to hear a proverbial pin drop if it hit the polished, cherry-wood floor.

He looked around at the familiar setting. He had been a regular at the café ever since he and Toni moved into the neighborhood almost thirty years ago. The food at Café Baci was a cut above the rest, but it was not the kind of place that you brought your wife and kids. Baci was for gentlemen only, a place to drink wine and smoke a cigar. The *No Smoking* law did not apply within the hallowed walls of Café Baci. It was a private club, a place to discuss business—by invitation only.

He heard the sound of footsteps and then the kitchen doors swung open. Giacomo Babocci had a tray of clean wine glasses on his shoulder as he entered the dining room. "Nick!" Babocci said with surprise. He set the tray down on the bar and rushed over to give his old friend a hug. He kissed him on both cheeks. "Nick, you son of a bitch, where have you been?"

"Maine," Sonellio replied. "At my cabin."

"You've got a cabin? I didn't know that. You hunt or fish?"

"Fish—they've got bass up there the size of tuna."

"*Madonna,* what about branzino?"

"Jaco, it's Maine, not the Mediterranean."

"No branzino?" Babocci said lightheartedly. "Ah, too

bad."

"Same old Jaco." Sonellio laughed, and then he coughed. His cough had become worse. Each cough was accompanied by a wheeze. It sounded like wind whistling through an old window.

"That's a bad cough you've got there, Nick. Bronchitis?"

Sonellio shrugged and framed a helpless expression. "Cancer."

"Oh Jesus Christ, Nick." Babocci grimaced. "You hit me right between the eyes with that one. Come here. Sit down for God's sake. Have a glass of wine."

Sonellio pulled out a chair and sat down at the closest table. Babocci inspected the wine rack and selected a bottle. He sat down at the table and proceeded to open the bottle with a corkscrew. "Tuscan Chianti," Babocci said. "A glass of this will fix you right up." He filled two glasses and slid one across the table to Sonellio. He lifted his glass and fanned the bouquet toward his nose. "What an aroma . . . like liquid fire."

"Here's to the good old days," Sonellio said as they toasted.

Babocci stared at Sonellio for a moment without talking. "You hungry, Nick? I'll have Alfredo whip you up a nice bolognese—how 'bout it?"

"Jaco, it's nine thirty. I just had breakfast."

Babocci's shoulders slumped. "I don't' know . . . you've made me very sad. What happened?"

"For God's sake, Giacomo, I've been smoking since the Eisenhower days. What the hell do you think happened?"

"They can't do anything for you?"

Sonellio took a mouthful of wine. "Nothing this Chianti can't do better." He put the glass down on the table and turned the base while he stared at it. "Jaco, you heard about the Jacoby family, yes?"

It took perhaps two seconds for Babocci to transform from a mellow restaurant proprietor into a raging, seething maniac. "Some motherfucker comes into our neighborhood and guns down an innocent family like that—it's a fucking disgrace. We're gonna get whoever it is, and we're gonna fix them good. It shows a total fucking lack of respect. The police have any solid leads?"

"No, we don't. That's why I'm here. I know that you've got your ear to the ground."

Babocci clenched his fist so tightly that his knuckles popped. He pointed at Sonellio. "I tell you one thing—if I do hear something, that piece of shit will be dead in a hurry. I guarantee it."

"Just calm down, Giacomo. You know they were my neighbors, right? I came home from Maine and saw that someone was using my backyard to case the neighborhood. I figured it was some crack addict looking to score some spare change, but I was wrong."

"You told the police?"

"Of course I told the police. I've devoted my entire career to law enforcement."

"And the Jacobys are dead anyway. You should've come to me—we would have found the prick before he did it."

"Giacomo, the whole thing happened in about ten minutes. Once I realized that someone had been in my yard, the police acted right away, but it was too late."

Babocci poured the glass of wine down his throat. "Like I said, it's a fucking disgrace. I knew those Jacoby boys; they were good kids." He sighed to evidence his extreme exasperation. "So what can I do for you, Nick? This has turned into a very bad morning."

"You know a lot of people, my friend. You haven't heard anything?"

"I'm gonna look, Nick. Believe you me, I will. I'll find something . . . trust me."

Sonellio flipped a business card on the table. "This is my old card, but the cell number is still good." He took a ballpoint pen out of his pocket and circled his cell phone number on the card. "I expect to hear from you if you find something—don't take matters into your own hands, *capisce?* These people were my neighbors, and I take their murders as a personal offense." He reached across the table and took Babocci's hand. "Come here," Sonellio said and pulled Babocci toward him. He kissed him on the cheek. "I'm not going to the grave in disgrace. Are we good?"

"Yeah, Nick, we're good," he said reluctantly. The two men stood and hugged.

"Remember," Sonellio said. "No vigilante shit. You bring this guy to me, and I'll fry him." For a brief moment, the disease had retreated into the background, and Sonellio was once again a force to reckon with. "You do this for me. Okay?"

"Yeah, okay, Nick." Babocci kissed Sonellio on the other cheek. "I'll bring you the motherfucker."

Chapter Twenty-nine

Rocco Sclafani sat in the funeral parlor parking lot, listening to the exhaust burble of his six hundred and sixty-two horsepower Shelby Mustang, sipping coffee. The funeral parlor was his by inheritance. His family had owned it for decades. He had grown up around the dead: draining blood and dressing corpses. He hated it, despite the money he made. He watched the clock. *Just two more minutes.* He revved the engine and listened to the growl of the immensely powerful engine. *Jesus, what the hell am I doing? I could sit here forever.* He shut the engine and walked to the building.

He unlocked the basement door and switched on the lights. The hot air from the cremation furnace hit him immediately. *What the hell?* The heat of the furnace imparted a distinctive arid quality to the air that he felt in his nostrils and lungs. He raced down the stairs and saw a red streak on the painted brick stairwell. He stopped and examined it for a moment. "Blood?" *Jesus, what's going on?*

He could hear the furnace roar as he approached. "I don't believe this." Sclafani knew that there were no bodies scheduled for cremation. He also knew that no one would be stupid enough to leave the furnace running unattended. He inspected the gauges on the outside of the furnace and then quickly shut the unit down. He peered through the viewing panel and saw a charred cremation container. "This is unbelievable," he said. "This is just un-fucking-believable."

Chapter Thirty

I was juggling a lot of balls at the same time. I was thinking about Ambler's case in one corner of my mind and the wanton murder of the Jacoby family in another. There was my pregnancy of course, absurdly high levels of hormones, my worries about Sonellio, a colossal appetite, erotic dreams, and let's see . . . was there anything else I had to concern myself with? No. I'd covered it. Needless to say I had a lot on my mind.

"I don't know how you can handle it all," Gus said. "I've got a migraine and *my* hormones are in check. Too bad you can't smoke pot."

"Smoke pot? Do I have to worry about you as well? Your back is better, isn't it? I hope this isn't going to become a way of life with you. If I wanted a pothead, I would have gone after Tully."

"I just found it relaxing, that's all. It's not like I do it every day."

I gave Gus a look that said, *tread lightly*. I didn't want him to become one of those fathers who sneak off to the bathroom to rock a joint while his kid is watching Sesame Street. "No more shit in your lungs, got it?" He nodded to confirm his understanding.

We were back in Staten Island. As if things weren't bad enough, we had just arrived at a funeral parlor. I mcan that was depressing in any respect, right? An unexplained body had been found in the furnace of the Sclafani Funeral Home. The owner, Rocco Sclafani, had found the body himself. He also saw blood smeared on the stairwell wall that led to the basement crematorium.

Richard Forzo, the Staten Island assistant chief, was waiting for us when we arrived. He was just outside the basement entrance speaking on his cell phone. We waited several minutes for him to end his call. "Where's Nick?" he asked.

"We gave him the day off," I said. "He's not feeling great. Toni called us and asked if we could give him a pass."

Forzo didn't look very happy. In fact, he looked as if he would have strangled someone if he could have gotten dispensation to do so. "There are days when this job just plain sucks. Today's one of those days." He straightened his back. "Is he getting worse?"

"I don't like what's happening to him," Gus said. "He's taking this Jacoby thing really hard. It's cutting him down fast."

"Shit!" Forzo looked off into the distance for a moment before turning back to us. "A crazy amount of crime has come down the pike in the last few days, and it's making me angry," he explained. "I mean the Jacoby murders are at the top of the list, but we've had a break-in at a pharmaceuticals company, and now this half-incinerated man. It's one thing on top of another. We usually get a lot of penny ante stuff, but crimes like these are pretty uncommon, and I don't like it when so much goes down at once."

Forzo was feeling responsible for the sudden spike in Staten Island crime, but for the most part, all the police could do was fix something after it was already broken. As much as we'd like to pat ourselves on the back, almost all of what we did was reactive and not proactive. "So what's going on here?" I asked. "A body was being incinerated?"

"Yeah," Forzo said. "The proprietor came in early this

morning and noticed that the furnace was running, even though there were no bodies scheduled for cremation."

"Do you think someone was incinerating a body to dispose of evidence?" Gus asked.

"That's my guess," Forzo said. "It's pretty crowded down there, but I want the two of you to take a look. There's something I know you'll find of interest. Shall we?" He turned and entered the building.

We followed him. He had broad shoulders. It almost looked as if they would touch the sides of the staircase as he descended. The smell of burnt flesh was just awful. The crime scene team had brought in fans to help move the air around. Even so, the odor was terrible. *Dig down deep, girl. Tough it out.*

The basement was chaotic with police crime scene investigators hovering around a charred body. A civilian stood in the center of the crowd. I assumed he was the proprietor. He was ranting like a lunatic. I suppose I couldn't blame the guy. Forzo made straight for him. Perhaps it was Forzo's size that caused the man to quiet down, which he did as soon as we approached. "Mr. Sclafani, I'd like you to meet Detectives Chalice and Lido."

"More detectives?" Sclafani asked. "There's only one burnt body. How many policemen do I need down here?"

"As many as it takes," Forzo said pointedly. "From the top, please tell these detectives everything that took place from the time you arrived this morning."

"Okay," Sclafani said. "It's just that this whole thing is driving me a little nuts." He reached out and shook our hands. "Rocco Sclafani," he said.

"Just another day at the office, huh?" Gus said. "Tell us what you found."

Oh dear God! I was now closer to the body than I wanted to be. *I don't mean to be callous, but did someone just barbecue an ox?* The victim was a huge man. He was so charred that it was impossible to look at the carcass for more than a few seconds. He looked like the roast that had been forgotten in the oven. My mind wandered, and I visualized the body in the furnace being consumed by flames. It was an image I hoped I would not retain.

"I got here early this morning," Sclafani said. "I wanted to make up the daily work schedule for the crematory operator before he got in."

"How early were you?" I asked.

"Almost an hour earlier than I usually get in," Sclafani said. "The first thing I noticed was that the furnace was running. That was the wake-up call. Then I saw that blood on the stairwell over there." He pointed to where a crime scene investigator was collecting a sample. The furnace is an older unit and the heat it throws off drives all the moisture out of the air. I could feel it in my nose and lungs as soon as I came in. There was no way that the furnace should have been running, but it was, so I knew something was wrong right away. I shut down the furnace as soon as I realized what was going on."

"How long does it take to cremate a body?"

Sclafani shrugged. "A guy this size? At least three hours, maybe more. This unit runs at about 1600 degrees Fahrenheit, but all of the moisture has to be driven out of the body before it gets that hot. A guy this size holds a lot of moisture. Figure one hour per hundred pounds." He looked down at the body. "This guy was a moose—three hours, easy."

"And how long do you think he was in there?"

"About an hour. The cremation container is made of plywood and cardboard which burns off almost immediately." He checked the victim again. "This body still contains some moisture. It's charred on the outside, but the internal organs haven't dried out sufficiently to combust."

"We found the charred remains of a wallet alongside the body," Forzo said. "The contents are pretty much destroyed, but the forensics lab may be able to piece together some information. Anyway, take a look over here. This is what I really wanted you to see." He motioned to a member of the crime scene unit. The investigator gently pulled down on the victim's jaw exposing the oral cavity. "From what you've told me you've seen dental work like this before."

"Son of a bitch," Gus said.

I forced myself to look into the victim's mouth. The incisors had been ripped out. I had already shared that aspect of our other investigation with Forzo. He'd put the pieces together immediately. I looked at the huge burnt body and knew that it was victim number three.

Chapter Thirty-one

I had not planned to spend the entire day in Staten Island but now that my two cases had been tied together . . . The Office of the Chief Medical Examiner was located at the Seaview Hospital Center. Gus and I grabbed an unoccupied office. We were discussing the two homicide cases and the new tie-in. I phoned Ambler to apprise him of the development. He was on his way across the Verrazano to join us. In the meantime, the forensic odontologist was having a field day examining the mouth of our rotund, charbroiled victim.

"You're going to think I'm crazy, but all of a sudden, I'm dying for the crispy beef at the Peking Duck House."

"You're a ghoul," Gus said. "How can you even think about food after seeing that body?"

"I'm not myself. Christ, I'm almost drooling."

"I think I'm going to become a vegetarian."

"Yeah, right, maybe for about ten minutes." I laughed. "One whiff of smoked sausage, and you'll be a goner." Gus loves his meat. Still, I could see how the body at the crematorium would leave quite an impression. I looked up and saw Ambler's broad profile filling the doorway. I smiled as he entered the office.

"Unexpected turn of events," Gus said.

Ambler shook his head and then stared at me. "How in God's name do you get involved in two completely separate, high-level investigations and tie them together?"

"Luck?" I said sheepishly.

"Luck my ass," Ambler said, "You're a witch, Chalice. How else can you explain it?"

Ambler didn't mean *witch* as in someone with warts and a pointy hat. He meant *witch* as in someone with supernatural powers, someone who knows things an ordinary person wouldn't know. "That's right, you nailed me, Herb. I looked into my cauldron this morning and foresaw the whole thing. By the way, that cauldron was filled with minestrone soup, and I'm getting hungry again."

"Dear God help me," Gus blurted.

"It's a good thing that Forzo is such a sharp number. Because of him we've been able to tie two Manhattan murder victims to an incinerated man in Staten Island. That's our first real break in this case."

"You call an unidentified incinerated man a break?" Gus said.

"Something ties these cases together. Our perp didn't select the Sclafani Funeral Home at random. He had to know the building. Not every funeral home offers cremation services. Our perp knew that, and he knew how to access the building and the furnace. I'm sure he also knew when Sclafani would arrive, and was in and out before he came to work. For all we know, victim number one may have been incinerated there as well and then the bones ground down to make the mortar for the tablet-shaped medallion."

"You're assuming of course that the victim we found in Kowsky Plaza and the victim you saw today were both butchered and murdered by the same perp," Ambler said. "We don't know that for sure. However, victim number two was identified. His name was Stuart Meisel, and he worked nearby at the Museum of Jewish Heritage."

"So both victims were Jewish."

"That's right. His parents reported him missing a couple of days ago."

"The MOs are completely different," Gus said. "One body was frozen and left for the authorities to find while today's victim was incinerated, presumably to dispose of the evidence."

"There's still the teeth, Gus. The killer doesn't need the body. All he needs is the teeth. He may be cementing them into a third medallion as we speak. I'll lay odds that today's victim will end up being number three."

"We should know something soon," Ambler said. "I had Marjorie send the FBI forensic file on the second victim to Forzo's forensic odontologist electronically so he'd have it to compare with today's victim."

"Speaking of Marjorie, anything going on between you two?"

"What is it with you, Chalice?" Ambler said. "Are you in perpetual ball-buster mode?"

"Only when I'm hungry." Ambler reached into his pocket and offered me his pack of gum. "What's that puny offering going to do? You'll have to do better than that." I pretended to sniff the air. "I think there's a pizzeria across the street."

"Oh dear God." Ambler turned away from me. "Gus, would you please take care of her before I lose my mind."

"She's always hungry," Gus said. "Food's not going to put an end to her incessant curiosity. So is there anything going on? Tell her before you and I are both forced to take our own lives."

"There's nothing going on," Ambler said emphatically.

"So you say." I winked at Ambler. "You're off the hook—here comes Michaelson, the odontologist."

"Assistant Chief Forzo asked me to bring you up to date," Michaelson said." He reached over, shook hands, and introduced himself to Ambler. He sat down at the head of the table and opened a folder. "I don't have a ton of information for you, but I can tell you that the same teeth were removed from both victims. The upper and lower gums were slit and the top and bottom incisors were ripped out, presumably with the use of pliers. Exactly eight teeth were removed from both victims, and they were all incisors."

"The perp has used teeth to form the numerals one and two. He inlays them into tablet-shaped medallions. I'm guessing that he uses the incisors because they're flat and easier to work with than the molars."

"So this is the third victim?" Michaelson asked.

"Presumably," Ambler said. "Tell us what you found."

"The victim was burned alive," Michaelson said. We all shuddered in unison. "You'll have to wait for the ME to do a complete examination of course, but I can tell you with certainty that the victim was alive because the oral cavity and descending air passages were completely lined with soot and ash. The victim was breathing at the time of death."

"Christ, that's awful." I'd seen Vetrov right after he had been pulled out of the furnace. It was tough enough to look at his partially incinerated body but to know he was burned alive . . . the thought was just horrible.

"Anything else?"

"The victim had a gold crown on one of his molars," Michaelson said. "Precious metals aren't used much these days because gold is so expensive. The cap was either put in several years ago or the work may have been done in Europe, where precious metal prosthetics are still more popular than synthetics." Michaelson closed his folder. "And that's all she wrote." He stood. "Anyone want to join me for lunch? There's a great pizzeria across the street."

Ambler's head spun toward me. He wore an expression of disbelief, which quickly became a smile. "Sure," he said. "The witch is buying."

Chapter Thirty-two

Rocco Sclafani turned out to be an all-right guy. I asked him to meet me at the police station, and he agreed to come right down. He was much calmer than he had been that morning. He obviously found perspective in the hours since we'd first met. He had changed his clothes and now wore a suit and tie. He looked like a completely different person.

"Hi, detective," he said as he sat down. "Just the two of us? Where's your partner and the commish?"

I shook hands with Sclafani. "My partner's at the crime lab and the commish, as you call him, is a busy man. BTW, he's the assistant chief of detectives, not a commissioner."

"I call every high-ranking cop 'the commish.' I used to watch that TV series with Michael Chiklis."

I noticed that Sclafani looked a little like Michael Chiklis. He was bald with a thick neck and broad cheekbones. "I saw it a few times. I liked his character." Almost every civilian believes that cops look and behave analogously with the characters they see week in and week out on their favorite TV shows—if they only knew the truth. "So *you* look different. Is this how you dress for work?"

"I'm a funeral director, Detective Chalice. I can't wear my jeans all the time. So tell me, *Cha-lee-see*, you're a *paesano*?"

"I am, brought up with a cross over my bed. I was baptized and went to catechism . . . the whole nine yards."

"Where are you from?"

"I'm a city girl. My father worked midtown north, like me."

"And now?"

"He's gone," I said, fighting the urge to get misty while I discussed the case with Sclafani. "God rest his soul."

Sclafani made the sign of the cross. "I'm so sorry. I lost my father too. Not long ago."

"Always lived on Staten Island?"

"Yeah, I was brought up around embalming fluid and caskets. Some childhood, huh?"

"You look like you turned out okay. Say, was that your Shelby Mustang I saw in the parking lot?"

Sclafani's eyes lit up. "That's my baby. It's the last one produced while Carroll Shelby was still alive—over six hundred and fifty ponies and a top speed of two hundred miles per hour."

"It's a gorgeous car."

"I take it out to the track—the car is an absolute beast."

"I assumed that you raced it. I saw a tow hook on your front bumper."

"Yeah, they make you do that so that they can drag you off the track if the car breaks down."

"Do you mind talking a little shop?"

Sclafani settled back in his chair. "No. Go ahead."

"So tell me what it takes to operate a cremation furnace?"

Sclafani smiled. "Can you roast a turkey?"

"So it's not hard?"

"No. My furnace is hardly state of the art, but the controls are completely electronic. It's no harder to incinerate a human body than it is to bake a casserole.

The controls are computerized and pre-programmed. All you have to do is prepare the body and slide it in. The furnace monitors the temperature and shuts down automatically when finished."

"You're telling me that anyone could have done it? You don't have to be specially trained to operate the furnace?"

"No. Don't get me wrong, detective, a crematory operator has to go through extensive training before he can be licensed, but most of the training has to do with the preparation of the body. The body has to be thoroughly examined before cremation. If the deceased has a pacemaker or other type of medical device, it has to be removed to prevent an explosion from occurring during the cremation process. After the remains are removed from the furnace, a powerful, hand-held magnet is run through the ash to pick up metal parts that might be left behind, such as fillings, plates, and prosthetic replacement joints, which can interfere with the grinding process."

"Grinding process?"

"The bones aren't reduced to ash. They have to be ground up."

"That's absolutely gruesome."

Sclafani shrugged. "What can I say? It paid for the Mustang."

"All right, so I'll need a list of all your current and former employees—not just the crematory operators, but anyone who worked for you and might have been able to operate the furnace."

Sclafani rubbed his eyes. "That will be a long list; my father opened the funeral parlor in 1965. A lot of the employees have come and gone—it takes a certain type of individual, if you know what I mean."

"Trust me, I get it. Let's start with the last five years.

I don't think we have to go back to the days of disco."

Sclafani chuckled. "Those were the good old days for me. You should've seen me on the dance floor. I made John Travolta look like he had arthritis."

"You're an impressive guy, Rocco."

"All the men in my family are good dancers."

I heard someone clearing his throat. I looked over my shoulder and saw that Gus had entered the room. "Is this a homicide investigation or an episode of *Who Do You Think You Are*?" Gus laughed and shook hands with Sclafani. "How are you, Rocco?"

"Better than this morning. I almost had a cow when I found that body this morning. I mean it's what I do for a living, but it was still a shock. I mean who does shit like that?"

"If we knew, we wouldn't be here," Gus said. "But this might help. The crime lab was able to pull the 2D barcode off the back of the incinerated driver's license found in the victim's wallet." He opened a folder and placed an enlarged copy of the drivers' license on the table. The man depicted had a large, round face, dark hair, and a beard. I could also see that one of his top incisor teeth was gold. The name on the drivers' license was Marat Vetrov. The deceased had a Brooklyn address.

I turned the printout so that Sclafani could see the face. "Ever see this man before?"

Chapter Thirty-three

He was looking at the driver's license when his throat tightened and he began to cough. I handed him a glass of water. "Take it easy, Brian. It's just a picture."

Brian Spano was a diminutive man. He looked like a boy lying in a standard-size hospital bed. He had a small frame and narrow shoulders. It was only the wrinkles and receding hairline that gave away his age. He took the cup of water from me and sipped through the straw. "Yeah," he said with an edge in his voice. "That's him." He began to cough nervously.

"Brian, calm down; he can't hurt you anymore."

"Okay." He took a few deep breaths. I gave him time to settle down.

I looked at the two pictures in my folder, Vetrov's driver's license photo and the sketch artist's rendering of the man who had attacked Spano. Forzo's squad was pretty damn sharp. They put two and two together and brought me the sketch of Spano's attacker as soon as it came in. The two images were close, but not that close. "You're sure that's him?"

"I'm positive. I'll never forget that face. It was the last thing I saw before I—" He reached for his neck and touched the support collar he was wearing. "I thought it was all over. I remember thinking, *this is it*! I thought I was about to die. I remember the look in his eye as he held me by the throat. Christ, I even remember his gold tooth. Do you believe that? I remember his stupid, gold tooth. I thought that I was going to die, and I noticed his tooth. Weird." Spano finished the water and put the empty cup on his tray. "So how did he die?"

"Someone broke his neck. His body was found in a funeral parlor cremation furnace."

Spano adjusted his pillow. "He got what he deserved."

"So let's run through your testimony again, okay?"

"Sure."

"You were doing a routine inventory. You saw cartons of pharmaceuticals on the floor, and then your assailant grabbed you by the throat."

"He shook me like I was a toy, detective. I was never so scared in my life."

"I'm sure it was pretty bad. You heard your neck snap, and you passed out."

"That's right."

"And you don't remember anything else until you came to at the garbage dump?"

"That's right."

"So no idea who brought you there or who rescued you from Vetrov?"

I could see in Spano's eyes that he wanted to remember. He was fighting to remember, but it just wasn't there. He seemed to be embarrassed. "I guess I was out the whole time. I'm sorry."

"You have my card. Hold onto it. You never know . . . something may come to you later."

"Forget it, detective," Spano said in a self-deprecating tone. "I'm not exactly a clutch hitter."

I could tell that Spano was feeling sorry for himself. Now I'm not a priest or a bartender, but I figured I could lend him a shoulder. "What's that supposed to mean?"

"My life's a mess, detective. I just got divorced." I saw his lips tighten. "I only get to see my son once every two weeks. I really want to come through for you, but the way my life is going . . . just don't expect too much, okay?"

Someone knocked on the door. I was still looking at Spano, and I could see the life return to his eyes. "Alex? Oh my God, buddy, come here." A woman and a little boy were standing in the doorway. I knew it was his wife and child. The woman let go of the boy's hand, and he ran over to Spano. He climbed onto the bed and into his father's arms. I saw tears in Spano's eyes as I stood.

"Things will get better, Brian," I said. "Keep your chin up." Spano smiled at me for a second and then turned back to his son. I introduced myself to his wife and then left the room. Spano was no hero, but he had been through a tough time. Sometimes things happened for a reason. Perhaps his assault . . . *I hope they get back together.* I didn't know if my little prayer would work, but it was worth a shot. Everyone deserves a second chance.

I bought a bottle of water from the vending machine. I figured the two of us needed some sorely needed hydration. I had chugged half the bottle when my cell phone rang. Herbert Ambler's name appeared on the caller ID. "What's up, my friend?"

"A third medallion just arrived at FBI headquarters, and it's tablet-shaped like the first two."

"And?" I was eager to hear the rest. I knew that it was something important.

"The numeral three is written out with incisor teeth and—"

"Well don't leave me hanging."

Ambler chuckled. "One of the teeth is gold."

Chapter Thirty-four

Tillerman unscrewed the top from the small bottle of medication and shook the remaining tablets into the palm of his hand. He stared at his trembling hand for a few seconds. His spasms had gotten much worse. They occurred more often and for longer lengths of time. He waited for the tremor to subside.

He was only taking six Repressor tablets a day, but there were seven left in the bottle. He dropped the empty bottle on the passenger seat of his van and threw the seven small tablets into his mouth. He crunched them between his teeth and washed them down with a swig of cold coffee. He no longer needed to worry about conservation. The big Russian had stolen thousands of tablets and now they were all his—enough to last for years.

"Now remember; just one pill per day." He chuckled as he remembered Dr. Schrader's warning. He had envisioned crushing Schrader in his powerful arms, pulverizing his ribs, and ending his life. He had dreamed about it—Schrader in his arms, his speech slowing until it finally stopped. The memory of the dream brought a smile to his face. Schrader's incessant nagging ate away at him, and the thought of his death made Tillerman feel peaceful. Schrader was meant to be the last of the four sacrifices.

He looked through the windshield of his van at the six-story apartment building just across the street. He imagined that he could see her window, the window she would sit in front of while she worked on her computers. Although he'd intended for Schrader to be the last, Kozakova's betrayal had catapulted her to the top of Tillerman's hit list. Her accomplice was dead, and she would be next.

Chapter Thirty-five

Giacomo Babocci kicked the kitchen door closed. He set an aluminum tray down on the table. "Tommy," he called out. "I'm home. I brought a nice tray of scaloppini home from the club. Hey, Tommaso, you hear me?" He took off his jacket and hung it on the back of a kitchen chair. "He's still downstairs?" he grumbled.

Babocci quickly looked around the ranch-style house and then took the stairs down to the basement. His son was sitting on the concrete floor, painting. Before him was a square, six-foot panel of glass, which was set into a metal frame and secured on either side to brick support columns. Every square inch of the glass was covered with paint. "Tommy, you didn't hear me call?"

Tom turned to greet his father. He had a content smile on his face. "Sorry, dad, I was lost in the moment."

Babocci smiled in return. It pleased him to see his son happy. Happy moments for his boy were few and far between. "So the glass is working out for you?"

"It's a great medium, dad, just like you said. I wish I had tried it sooner. The brush moves across the glass effortlessly." He set down his brush and pushed back with his right arm to move out of the way and give his father a full, unobstructed view of his work. It was a landscape of a large, weathered house set near the ocean. "What do you think?"

Babocci stepped back so that he could get a better perspective. "I love the colors, especially the blue."

"That's cobalt, dad." The house was painted in

shades of cobalt and white. Tom had achieved a very dramatic rendering of the old house and the ocean. His skill with the brush was first rate.

"And you used the pointillism technique throughout?" Tom nodded. "Seurat and Georges Lemmen used that method frequently. It's a lot of work but the result speaks for itself." He kissed the tips of his fingers. "Incredible work, Tommy, I was never this good." Babocci looked more closely. He stared at the dark areas and the light. When he focused on the painting he could see that the dark areas had a dense concentration of dots. The concentration of paint dots in the lighter areas were much more diffused. "Just great, and the way the shadows play on the old house . . . I love it." Babocci never cried in front of his son, but he ached to do so. Every moment with his son tore at him; a tug of war between thankfulness and torment. "I'm starving. How about you?"

"Hell yes. I haven't eaten all day."

Babocci extended his hand. "I'll help you up."

"No thanks. I'm good." Tom pushed down on the floor with his right hand to lift his torso and then stood on his right leg. He didn't put weight on his prosthetic left leg until he was almost completely vertical. He took a moment to inspect his artwork. He got right up against the painting and stared at the dark window as if he were looking into the house.

"Everything all right?"

"Just being my meticulous, neurotic self."

Tom turned to face his father. A shadow illuminated him in the worst possible light. Babocci saw the gathered waistband of his son's jeans and the end of his belt that hung over his damaged hip and decimated left leg. He fought the impulse to gasp. His son had gone off to war in the Persian Gulf and returned half a man. The left side of his son's body had been destroyed in an enemy offensive. His left arm had been removed in an army hospital operating room along with his lower leg. "How are you doing today?"

"I'm fine, dad. I'm home two years already—you don't have to ask me every day." He put his right arm on his father's shoulder, and they began to walk side by side.

"You're doing good," Babocci said. "I can barely feel you limp."

"I only limp when I'm tired, dad. I walk over two miles every day."

"Two miles? *Madonna.*" Babocci pinched his son's cheek. "You're in better shape than I am. Let's go upstairs and stuff ourselves on Alfredo's veal."

"What about dessert?"

"I brought home half of a pizza grana." He kissed his fingertips again. "*Delizioso.*"

"Thanks, dad, you've been like a father *and* mother to me ever since—"

Babocci held up his finger to silence his son. He made the sign of the cross. "It's okay, son. It's okay."

Chapter Thirty-six

There are times when it was okay to be indulgent and times when you have to forsake the sweet tooth and break a sweat. This was one of those times. I was shoulder to shoulder with my brother Ricky as we ran along the FDR Drive. Running next to Ricky was like running alongside a racehorse. He was silent and strong, rarely speaking when we ran. He wasn't there to keep me company. He was there to look out for his pregnant sister. He would catch me looking at him every now and then—just quick glances from the corner of my eye—adoring glances because I loved Ricky for who he was.

"You okay, sis?"

"Yup," I always kept it simple and sweet, and then I would tease him by pulling ahead and forcing him to catch up. He would catch me every now and again, and I would respond with the same one word affirmation and another burst in speed. I laughed on the inside every time, and then my heart would ache for a moment because . . . I wondered what he was thinking in that simple but beautiful mind of his. I wondered if he understood what had happened to him. Did he remember how he was before? Did he remember being a high school football sensation? Did he yearn to be more? Did he hope to get better, or did he just live in the here and now? I didn't know which was better for him. I only wanted him to be happy. *I love you, Ricky.*

"What? Did you say something?"

Only that I love you. "I'm thirsty." I saw a hotdog cart up ahead. We ran up to it and stopped. I bought two bottles of water. We sat down on a bench and drank as we looked across the river.

"What's over there?" he asked.

"Queens."

"How do you get there?"

He had such a good heart. He wouldn't let his armed policewoman sister go for a run unless he could go along as a chaperone. He had lived in Manhattan for years and still didn't . . . or couldn't . . . there were boats in the water, and the RFK Bridge was off in the distance . . . but he couldn't connect the dots. Nigel was working with him, helping him to improve. Ricky had made some moderate strides, but his issues with disassociation persisted. I pointed off into the distance. "You can drive over that bridge. If you look closely you can see cars on it."

"Oh yeah." He took a sip from the water bottle and wrinkled his nose. "This water smells funny."

"I think you smell the East River. It's humid today."

He looked at me with a blank expression. "What's humid?"

"Ah, come on, Ricky. You know what humid means. There's a lot of moisture in the air."

He smiled with one side of his mouth. I had learned that he did that when he was embarrassed. "Oh yeah, that's right."

We both became quiet as we stared out at the water. Whatever Ricky was thinking about, it wasn't the wanton murder of an innocent family, and he certainly wasn't thinking about the body of a man who had been burned alive in an incinerator. One day soon, Gus and I would have a family of our own. Yes, we were cops, but no one can be alert all the time. There are so many monsters out there. Who would keep an eye out for us? What would prevent another tragedy like the one that happened to the Jacoby family? Maybe Ricky was the smart one. Perhaps his was the better way. Somehow though, despite being incredibly naïve, he felt a need to protect me. I felt like crying but really didn't want to. I tousled his hair instead. "Thanks for keeping me company."

"It's okay. I like running. Can we run all the way over to Queens?"

"If we get in really fantastic shape, but I don't think I'll be ready for that anytime soon."

"Because of the baby?" Ricky grinned from ear to ear.

"Yes, because of the baby. Are you excited about the baby?"

He nodded. "I want to be an uncle."

"You'll be a great uncle." *Even when the baby goes to school and . . .* My throat tightened. *Even when . . .* "Because I know you'll love the baby so much."

"I love it already. Even though I can't see it."

I had been thinking about the case while we ran. I found that exercise inspired me, but I still had not been able to associate the latest elements of the case. Marat Vetrov attacked Brian Spano while he was taking inventory at the pharmaceuticals plant, and Vetrov had subsequently been murdered. I guess I hadn't run far enough, because I hadn't been able to connect those two events. I knew that the connection was there, just off in the horizon.

"Gus is with you when you work, isn't he?"

"Why do you ask, Ricky?"

He shrugged. The one-sided smile came back. "Just because."

"Well, Gus is my partner at work so we do a lot of

things together."

"But not everything?"

"No, Ricky, not everything."

"Maybe you should."

"Are you worried about me because I'm going to have a baby?"

Ricky nodded. "There's safety in numbers," he said, parroting something he must have heard someone else say. "Someone robbed the store where I work, but I wasn't there."

"Someone robbed the paint store?"

"Yeah. They took a lot of money, and the owner hired a security guard. Maybe you should hire a security guard to watch you when Gus can't be around."

A security guard? The idea rolled around in my head for a moment. Could that be the connection I'd been looking for? "You're so smart. Don't worry. Your sister can take care of herself."

"You're smarter than me, Stephanie."

I kissed Ricky on his sweaty forehead. "No I'm not, but right now I have a bigger appetite. Come on, I'll race you home."

Chapter Thirty-seven

"**Are** you sure all of this running is good for you?" Ma said. "I never ran."

I plopped down on her couch as Ricky headed off to the shower. Ma opened a Ziploc bag and handed me a slice of honey baked ham. "Yes, I'm sure it's good for you."

"You're positive? Because I don't see a lot of pregnant women jogging."

"Trust me, I checked with Dr. Kranston, and he said it was okay. Besides, it was just a light run. I didn't run a marathon."

"Why don't you try one of those exercise bikes?"

"Uh, because they're boring, and I enjoy running." I snatched the bag of cold cuts out her hand and reached in for a second slice. I had called Gus on the run back to Ma's and was waiting for him to check out the security-guard angle—A secure facility like Vicor has hundreds of security cameras. I'm sure that someone had monitored Vetrov's attack on Brian Spano, and I wanted to know who it was. I checked my phone to make sure that I hadn't missed any calls.

"Okay, forget all of that," Ma said. "How about I whip up a quick batch of macaroni with peas?"

Yes! Oh God, yes. I smiled. "That's exactly what I want."

"I just got a chuck of Romano cheese—we'll grate it fresh. How soon before Gus gets here?"

"Could be a while—he's checking on something for

me."

"Those awful murders in Staten Island? Poor Nick, he must be crushed."

I had not seen Sonellio in a couple of days. On the one hand, I wanted him to get a few days rest, but on the other hand, I was afraid to see if he had gotten any worse.

"Silly man. I can't remember him without a cigarette in his mouth. You never smoked, right?"

"Ma! How can you ask a question like that? You know how I feel about smoking."

"Well now, sure . . . I mean when you were a teenager. All kids sneak cigarettes."

"No. Never." I may have snuck an occasional boyfriend into the house, but she didn't ask, and I was not about to volunteer information. Not that it mattered anymore—in fact, we would probably have a good laugh over it.

"You're telling the truth?"

"Yes!"

"Okay, I believe you," Ma had a wise-ass grin on her face. "But I know about you and Frankie Bono."

Oh shit. Here it comes.

"What are you talking about?" My words of innocence didn't matter—I could feel that I had one of those *cat who ate the canary* expressions on my face.

"Don't you BS me, Stephanie Marie Chalice. I knew all about it."

Wow . . . and Ambler called *me* a witch—now I knew where it came from. Should I deny it? Nah, what the hell for? I grinned. "How did you know?"

"Do you think I was born yesterday? Do you think I didn't see what they wrote about you in your high school yearbook? *Bright and beautiful, she always makes the scene, but look out boys, she's Frankie's queen.*"

"Jesus, you saw that?"

She chuckled. "Saw it? Your father and I had some of our biggest laughs over it."

I turned to look in the mirror. I was beet red. "So why didn't you say something?"

"Because you broke up with him soon afterward." She grinned again. "But I knew."

She knew? How could she have known? I was a cop's daughter—I'd always been careful to cover my tracks. Since a strong offense was the best defense, I said simply, "You're full of it."

"Yeah, *I'm* full of it?"

"You don't know anything. You're making it up." I laughed so hard that it hurt.

"You think you and your father were the only detectives in the house? It rubs off, you know. I've got you dead to rights."

"Seriously?"

"Francine Delgado's mother told me all about it. Francine used to follow the two of you home from school every day. She had such a crush on Frankie. Her mother said that she used to cry herself to sleep every night."

"Francine Delgado?"

"Yes."

"Little Francine with acne?"

"Yes!"

"No wonder she hated me."

"Don't feel too bad. She just married a football player, someone on the New York Jets."

"You're kidding?"

"Well, it's true. She must've found a good dermatologist, because I saw her wedding picture and she looked beautiful."

"Really? That's nice. I'm so happy for her."

"Speaking of marriage, when are you and Gus going

to make it official?" She narrowed her gaze. "You're wasting time."

Gus and I had talked about it but just hadn't yet put a plan into action. Working two homicide cases didn't help. "Soon."

"You'd better make it *very* soon, before Francine Delgado's mother starts calling you the *puttana* cop."

My mouth dropped. "She wouldn't?"

"Oh yes she would. That woman carries a grudge like no one else, and she knows how to gossip. You made her daughter miserable, and I think she wants revenge."

"Oh let her talk. Who cares?"

"I care. You don't live in the neighborhood anymore. You think I want to hear things like that?"

I supposed Gus and I had better take care of business before Ma became collateral damage in the mid-Manhattan gossip wars. As I said, it was already on our agenda. I heard a knock on the door. "That's probably Gus. You can ask him yourself."

Ma followed me to the front door. "I also found Frankie's bus pass when I was cleaning your bedroom one day." She gave me a pat on the fanny. I could see that she was all worked up. "Open the door. I'm going to let Gus have it, both barrels."

I pulled the door open. Gus knew that he was in trouble at the first sight of Ma's face. It read like a HazMat warning. "What's wrong?" he said.

"Are you going to marry me or what?" I demanded. "People are starting to talk."

"Talk about what? Who's talking?" Gus looked somewhat flustered.

"You're in deep shit," I chuckled. "Mrs. Delgado called me a *puttana.*"

"She what?"

"The talk around town is that I'm a big slut."

Ma began to howl. "It didn't help any that you and Frankie Bono played grab-ass in the twelfth grade." Gus looked at us as if we had lost our minds. Ma grabbed Gus by the arm and pulled him into the apartment. "Get in here, mister; we need to have a pow-wow."

I closed the door, but I knew that the neighbors could hear us laughing all the way down the hall.

Ma pointed to the couch. "Sit down. Macaroni and peas okay for dinner?" she asked. Gus nodded. "Give me two minutes—I'll put up a pot of water."

I grabbed Gus and yanked him down onto the couch. "You knew this was coming. I guess you'd better make me an honest woman."

Gus made an expression that said, *yeah right.* "So who's this Frankie Bono character? I'm not going to marry you now," he said facetiously. "You're used goods."

I laughed so hard that it was difficult for me to switch gears. "Quick. Before she gets back, anything on the security guard angle?"

"Yeah, you were right." That was all that Gus managed to say before Ma came back into the room. Vetrov had to have been there for the drugs, and I was betting whoever took him down was there for the same reason. I was betting that a crosscheck on patients for Vicor's trial drugs and security guards who worked at Vicor's warehouse would be quite revealing.

"You think I'm going to live forever?" Ma said dramatically. "I'm an old woman with diabetes. How long do I have to wait to see my darling daughter walk down the aisle?"

I was still in a silly mood. I glared at Gus. *"Well?"*

Gus was caught in the proverbial crossfire. "We can have a quick civil ceremony as soon as we wrap up our cases."

It took perhaps a nanosecond for the avalanche to fall on him. “You don’t understand,” Ma said with outrage. “My daughter is not going to have a civil ceremony. My daughter is going to get married *in church with bridesmaids and flowers.*”

Gus looked to me for support, but there was no defense against my mother’s onslaught. He sat there and took it like a man.

Chapter Thirty-eight

Tillerman stood outside the entranceway of the Staten Island medical examiner's office for a few moments to rehearse his performance. He had been in this position before, years ago when he worked for the funeral parlor. He knew the drill. *Stay calm. Act natural.* He pushed the door open and walked up to the reception counter. A mature woman wearing glasses with blue frames looked up from her computer screen. "Sclafani Funeral Home," he said and handed her completed release forms. "We called ahead for a pickup." He was dressed in jeans. He wore a nylon jacket that was embroidered with the Sclafani emblem.

The receptionist reviewed the paperwork and then checked her watch. "It's lunchtime. I don't know if anyone's back there to help you."

Of course it's lunchtime. That's why I'm here. "There's always someone on the floor. They never leave the morgue unattended."

The receptionist smiled. "I guess this isn't your first trip to the rodeo."

"Nope. I know the ropes," Tillerman said with a smile.

She picked up the phone. "Let's just see if I can get one of the technicians to help you. I think Jeffrey might still be here." She checked the directory, hit the speaker setting, and then punched in an extension number.

"Morgue." The voice at the other end of the line sounded young to Tillerman. He smiled again.

"Jeffrey, it's Claire. Sclafani is here for a pickup. Can you come out and help?"

Jeffrey burped on the other end of the line. "Oops, sorry, Claire. I'm eating at my desk."

"Taco Bell?"

"No, Mickey D's. I'll be right there."

Claire hung up the phone. "Nice young man, but he eats the most god-awful stuff.

"Fast food," Tillerman said. "We're all guilty." He was doing a great job of being congenial, despite the fact that his stomach was churning with anxiety. His hand trembled and then locked in spasm momentarily. He began to rub the area between the palm and thumb.

Claire noticed the tremor. "Are you all right, dear? It looks like you're in pain."

"It's nothing," Tillerman said. "Occupational hazard."

"Oh, just like me—I've got carpal tunnel. Do you do a lot of typing?"

"The paperwork is endless," Tillerman replied. "The state drives us crazy with red tape."

"I know, it's awful, isn't it?"

Tillerman nodded. He turned when he heard the release of an electric door lock. A man who looked to be in his twenties approached the reception counter. He held his security tag in one hand and a milkshake in the other. Tillerman grinned when he saw him. The position of morgue technician was an entry-level job. No experience was needed, just a high-school diploma. *Perfect. Absolutely perfect.*

Claire waved an admonishing finger at him. "Jeffrey, you'll get fat."

"No worries, Claire," he replied. He picked up the paperwork and began to look through it. He glanced up at Tillerman. "Four bodies—I'm glad they sent someone big. I hope you didn't bring a hearse."

Tillerman shook his head. “No. I’ve got a van with slide out trays. I can fit them all.”

“Great,” Jeffrey said. “Let’s do it.”

Chapter Thirty-nine

Gus had a bellyful of pasta and his foot on the gas. We were once again on our way to Staten Island, and Gus was happy as hell to have gotten out of Ma's apartment with just a light beating. "What the hell was that?" he said. "You couldn't have given me a head's-up?"

I began to laugh. "I'm sorry. I know it's not funny. It was all happening right there and then. You walked through the door and got it right between the eyes." I continued to laugh. "I'm really sorry."

"Jesus, I thought she was going to disembowel me."

"Well what do you want, hot stuff? You got her sweet, innocent daughter in a family way. That can't go unpunished."

"You're nuts, do you know that?" The Verrazano Bridge was coming into view. "So tell me about you and this Frankie guy." Gus gave me a probing stare. "You were doing him in high school?"

"No. It was just adolescent stuff: making out, petting, groping—you've been there. We'd watch TV, he'd cop a feel, and so on and so on. He never got past second base. Ma knows it too or she would have shut it down in a heartbeat. She trusted me and I would never let her down."

"The poor guy must have had a serious case of blue balls."

"Hey, I was brought up as a good Catholic girl. If Frankie had to go home and do a load by hand . . . well, so be it. Believe me, there were lots of guys who wanted to slide their hands up my blouse. Frankie was the envy of all his friends—he told me so."

The thump of the tires on the Verrazano's approach grid cued me to focus my attention back onto the case. Our records search had turned up a match. It was well after hours, and it took me several calls to track down the suspect's employer and get the address reported on his employment records. We were on our way to that address. "How long did this guy Tillerman work for Sclafani?"

"He was there almost three years. According to Sclafani, he didn't operate the furnace, but he spent enough time in the basement to pick up on how to operate it."

"And he's been working security ever since?"

"No. He was off the grid for a while. He's only been with the security company for about six months."

"Hard to believe a big company like Vicor doesn't have its own security team. I mean it's the pharmaceuticals industry. I'm sure they spend a fortune to prevent industrial espionage."

"Oh, they have corporate security up the yin-yang, but they hire Beacon to do the nuts and bolts stuff," Gus said. "You know, they sit at the reception area after hours and monitor the closed-circuit TV. They patrol the parking lot . . . They can't actually enter the facility. They're strictly outsiders."

Something Gus said struck me. It took a moment for it to sink in. "Did you say Beacon Security?"

"Yeah, why?"

An image flashed in my head. I pictured a security guard asleep at his post. The emblem on his jacket read Beacon Security. "You didn't happen to ask Beacon where else Tillerman has been assigned, did you?"

"No."

"Beacon Security covers the pumping station we visited at Kowsky Plaza in Lower Manhattan. I remember seeing the name on the security guard's jacket." My skin began to tingle. "My God, we're so close."

It must have been the close proximity to Sonellio's home that made me think of him. He was a cop to the very end. He was staring at the grave and yet wanted nothing more than justice for his neighbors. I ached for him and planned to phone him first thing in the morning to brief him on Tillerman, our new suspect. I wondered if we'd be able to give him closure before . . . I sighed.

We were off the boulevard. Gus directed the car down a narrow side street. He checked the address he had written on his notepad. "There it is, on the right."

I looked up at the sky through the windshield. It was the most beautiful shade of navy blue. Puffs of clouds like dabs of white paint obscured my view of the moon. An old street light sputtered on and off. There was little light, but it wasn't hard to tell that the house we had come to visit had been boarded up. I felt my heart sink. "Damn."

Gus pulled up in front of the small home and turned off the engine. We each grabbed a Maglite and got out of the car to take a look.

Chapter Forty

Tatiana was *the* place to go on a Saturday night if you were a Russian living in Brooklyn. The supper club featured fine dining, dancing, and a show. The patrons dressed to the nines. Vodka flowed like water. Russians are always thirsty.

Anya Kozakova sat at a table for ten, but she was the only one not up on the dance floor. She lifted a bottle of vodka out of a block of ice and poured the last of it into her glass. "Here's to me," she said sadly. "At least I'm out of the apartment." The house band was loud. The vocalist had dark hair, a widow's peak, and a groomed beard. He wore a bright blue taffeta tuxedo jacket. He sang in Russian while the band covered a popular tune, "*япоцеловалдевочкаиялюбилего,*" which loosely translated into "I kissed a girl and I liked it."

Kozakova hummed the song, accompanying the vocalist. The fresh hit of vodka topped off her buzz. Her mind was numb and quiet. It was the first time in days that she was not thinking in computer code.

Her friend Olga saw her and walked off the dance floor. Olga was a tall blond. She had legs like Cameron Diaz and wore a dress short enough to show off every inch of them. She plopped down in the chair next to Kozakova and began to massage her feet. "These shoes are killing me," she said. "That's what I get for buying cheap knockoffs."

"Cheap knockoffs maybe, but every man out there wants to dance with you," Kozakova said. "You have gorgeous legs."

"Thank you," she said. "Where is your big, fuzzy friend, Marat? He's usually here."

"I thought he was coming but . . . you know men. He's probably passed out drunk somewhere. I can only count on seeing him when he's horny."

"Speaking of horny, why don't you dance with that single guy over there. He's dancing with a couple. Open your top button and shove your big breasts in his face."

"Which one?" Kozakova said as she turned toward the dance floor.

Olga pointed to a tall, thin man with wire-rimmed glasses and a mustache.

"Him? The one who looks like Nietzsche? You must be joking."

"What's wrong with him?" Olga protested defensively. "Better you should sit here alone?" She picked up the closest glass of vodka and toasted Kozakova. "Go, Anya, the night is long—better to go home with a homely man than to go home alone." She whispered in her ear, "A vibrator may get you off, but it won't keep you warm." Olga laughed and then stood up. "Come on, the singer has a great voice. I love Nicki Minaj." She quickly walked back to the dance floor.

Kozakova swallowed the rest of her vodka and stood up without thinking about a plan or consequences. She undid the top button of her blouse as Olga had instructed and made her way over to the dance floor. She arrived just a few seconds too late. By the time she located the Nietzsche look-alike, he was dancing with someone else.

The club's main entrance was located on the Riegelmann Boardwalk at Brighton Beach. Kozakova walked out onto the boardwalk, leaned against the railing, and looked out at the Atlantic. Wind rushed north, and she was only able to take the chill for a few minutes before she headed home. She was mildly disappointed with the evening, but the vodka was doing its job, and there was more of it waiting for her at home. She had just turned onto Brightwater Court when Tillerman came up behind her and pounded down on her skull with his massive fist. She collapsed, and he dragged her into his van.

Chapter Forty-one

I called for assistance. The entrances and first-floor windows were boarded up. We would need a tactical team to gain access to Tillerman's home. It didn't stop us from taking a look around—if there was a quick way in, we'd find it. I walked around the side of the house to the back. The entrance to the cellar was a sloped wooden door. It had been boarded up as well, but I pulled on one of the boards and was able to yank it free. With the board out of the way, I could see the padlock that secured the door. *Piece of cake.* "Gus," I called out.

It took a second for Gus to emerge out of the shadows. "Find something?"

I illuminated the exposed padlock with my searchlight beam. "We've got a bolt cutter in the trunk, don't we?"

Gus smiled. "You bet." He walked off and returned a minute later with a large bolt cutter. I focused the searchlight beam on the padlock while he cut the shackle. Boards were nailed over the door. They gave way when Gus pulled on it.

"Great, nothing like crawling around a creepy, dark basement. Can't think of anything I'd rather do." I focused the searchlight beam on the steps and descended. I walked right into a huge spider web. As soon as I cleared the web away, I noticed a light switch and tried it, but the power was off. The basement was pitch black. I explored the darkness. The basement was unfinished, cinderblock walls and a concrete floor. I saw a large, steel cart at the far end of the basement. I walked closer and saw that it was a necropsy table, a table designed for working on cadavers. Like most, this one had a plastic runoff tube through which the cadaver's blood could drain. It ran a few feet to a slop sink, which was stained red.

Gus walked over to the sink and examined it with his searchlight. "I'll get a crime scene team down here. It looks like there's some dried blood around the drain."

"Good deal." I continued to look around and saw a wooden cabinet. I opened the doors and found a clean set of necropsy instruments and several jugs of embalming fluid. Gus walked over to show me a handful of small, white, conical objects that he was holding. "Trocar buttons?"

"I found a bag of them under the necropsy table."

Trocar buttons are threaded plugs an ME uses to seal the wound he's made to fill the internal cavity with embalming fluid. "Why is he embalming them?" I asked. "It's not consistent with his MO. We're not sure what really happened to the first victim, but we know that Tillerman ground up his bones to make a medallion. The second victim was found intact but frozen, and Tillerman tried to incinerate the third victim. I'm confused."

Gus seemed equally perplexed. He bit off a hangnail and then shrugged.

I heard the sound of a car pulling to a stop outside the house. "Sounds like reinforcements are here. I can't wait to explore the rest of this dirty old sarcophagus."

Herbert Ambler came down the basement stairs a moment later. Marjorie Banks followed him. I mused that they were out on a date when they got the call to head over our way. I took one look at Ambler's face and knew better. The four of us were holding searchlights—

they threw off enough light for Ambler to take in the scene before him. He looked down at the trocar buttons in Gus' hand and looked up with an expression of puzzlement on his face. "What the hell?"

"I know, not what you expected, right? We're confused also."

"It doesn't fit the unsub's MO," Banks said. BTW, Marjorie wore a very well cut jacket and black slacks. She looked thin and chic. I'm sure Ambler noticed her appearance as well—at least I hoped he had.

"We were just saying that. There's a cabinet filled with embalming fluid over there. Embalming equipment is the last thing I expected to find."

"I'll have the building pulled apart for clues. Any leads as to where this guy Tillerman might be?" Ambler asked.

"He hasn't shown up for work since the night the pharmaceuticals company was robbed," Gus said. "He's MIA."

"There's a big goddamn surprise," Ambler said. "Do we have a line on the meds that were stolen from Vicor? Anything show up on the street?"

"It was all experimental stuff," I said. "Antidepressants, antipsychotics, anxiety meds . . . not the kind of drugs we'd hear about even if they did end up on the street. I'm not quite sure what this Russian guy, Vetrov, wanted with them."

"Industrial espionage?" Banks suggested.

"Very possible," Ambler replied. "Who knows who Vetrov was working for. Russian drug trafficking has become huge over the last several years, but that's more about narcotics. Pharmaceutical espionage is an entirely different ball of wax. I'll check with the CIA, but the chances are they won't reply, even if they know something."

"Why can't we all just get along?" Gus said.

Ambler gave Gus a smug smile. "Pipe down, will ya? Who do you think you are, Rodney King?"

Gus gave Ambler the old *F-U, I'm pretending to wipe a tear from my eye* gesture.

"Okay, boys, settle down." I turned to Ambler. "You okay if we leave? I want to hit the computer to check background on Tillerman and Vetrov."

"It's one in the morning," Ambler said. "Don't you and the fetus need some rest?"

Marjorie scowled at Ambler and gave him a playful slap on the wrist. "What kind of talk is that?"

"Sorry," Ambler said and smiled at her. It was more than a smile actually—to a cop like me it was a smoking gun. "We know each other a long time."

"It's okay, Marjorie, I bust his chops all the time. Don't worry, Herb. I'm not tired."

"Sure," Ambler said. "Take off. Call me if you come across anything juicy."

"Will do."

We had not quite reached the car when Gus grabbed my arm. "You think something is going on with those two?"

"I don't know but that slap on the wrist got my suspicions going. Did you see the smile he gave her? That smile said, *I want to jump your bones.*"

"Marjorie looks good tonight."

See? I'm not the only one—Gus noticed too. "I sure hope that spark catches fire. I want to see those two together almost as much as I want to solve this case."

"I think you're getting a little ahead of yourself, Stephanie. They just met."

"You never know, Gus. Maybe we'll have a double wedding."

Chapter Forty-two

The first sensation Anya Kozakova had upon regaining consciousness was that she was suffocating. Both eyes shot open in panic. Tillerman allowed her panic to grow for a moment before he grinned and reached behind her to release the valve on her scuba tank. Dry pressurized air instantly filled her lungs. Her fear of suffocation subsided and was immediately replaced with newly realized panic. She was eye to eye with Tillerman on a small boat surrounded by water in the middle of the night. She tried to move but couldn't. Her arms were taped together in front of her. Her ankles were bound in the same manner. The scuba tank bindings pulled snugly across her chest. She tried to push the regulator out of her mouth with her tongue, but it was designed to fit snuggly and could only be pulled out by hand.

Tillerman grasped the regulator and pulled it out of her mouth. "Better?"

Kozakova nodded nervously. Her breathing was rapid. She tried to fill her lungs with fresh air and calm down, but the situation was too extreme. She began to hyperventilate.

Tillerman slapped her across the face with an open hand, just hard enough to focus her attention. "Relax. I have questions." He stood and walked to the other side of the small fishing boat. He picked up a weighted diver's belt. "Stand up," he ordered.

Kozakova tried to comply, but she was in a state of

full-blown panic and was unable to stand with the scuba equipment on her back. Tillerman grabbed her under the arm and yanked her to her feet. He weighed the heavy belt in his hand before he fastened it around her waist.

Kozakova reached down deep and found her courage. She was an honest–to-God tough girl and was determined not to cower before her assailant. "You're going to drown me? Why?" she demanded. "What did I do to you?"

Tillerman considered her question for a moment before he responded. "Why did you betray me?"

"Betray you? What are you talking about? I haven't thought about you even once since you left my apartment. How? How did I betray you?"

"As if you don't know."

"Oh fucking Christ, man. I didn't do anything. Are you crazy? I altered your security tag so that you could access all areas of the pharmaceuticals building—that's all."

"And you made a copy for your friend."

"My friend? What friend?"

"Med-ved," he said, recalling the phonetic pronunciation of the word he had learned from her. "The big grizzly bear . . . like me."

Kozakova's mind raced to decipher the puzzle and then her eyes widened. "Marat?"

"Yes, Marat," he repeated. "I took good care of him."

It took a moment for her to understand what Tillerman meant, but then recognition registered on her face. "You killed him?" Marat was dead, but she was too invested in her own self-preservation to worry about him. "Marat's a sneaky fuck. He must have stolen my encryption key and made a copy of the security pass. Honestly, what the hell do you think I had to do with it?

I don't even know what they have in that stupid building."

"They have clinical test medications like Repressor, the one I take every day."

"I don't know what that is."

"It's my happy pill. It gets me through the day—one day at a time. It also keeps me from snapping people's necks . . . well, most of the time. I did snap your friend's neck, but he deserved it. He stole my meds and almost killed a tiny, little man, but I caught up with him and set things right."

Kozakova sighed. It was a deep and troubled sigh, one that communicated her extreme exasperation. "I told you I didn't do anything. If you want your money back, you can have it. You want my body? You can have that too."

"You're a liar and a con artist."

"Fuck you! I work like a dog all day long. My only mistake was to help an idiot like you. I thought you were strong." She arched her neck. "Go ahead, snap my neck. I don't want to drown."

"You won't." Tillerman looked her in the eye and then forced the regulator back into her mouth. He ran tape around her head to hold it in place. It was the same heavy-duty, water-resistant tape he'd used to bind her wrists and ankles. He watched the courage disappear from her face and her eyes fill with terror. He checked the gauge on the pressure regulator and the lines that led to her buoyancy control vest. He closed his eyes. "Blessed are the elements of life. May the air consume you." He opened his eyes and pushed her into the ice-cold waters beneath the Verrazano Bridge.

Chapter Forty-three

Toni Sonellio heard the doorbell ring. She wasn't expecting company and walked to the front door to see who it was. She pulled aside the shear curtain and looked through the glass panel that bordered the door. She recognized the man standing outside her home as one of her husband's acquaintances but could not remember his name. She unlocked the door and opened it. "Hi, I know we've met before, but—"

"Giacomo Babocci," the man offered. "I'm Nick's friend from Café Baci over on the avenue. Is he home?" He held out a foil-wrapped baker's tray.

"What's this?" Toni said posting a polite smile.

"I brought you a nice tiramisu—baked fresh."

"Thank you. Come in," Toni said as she made room for Babocci to enter. "My husband has a real sweet tooth. He'll enjoy this."

"Why sure," he said in a matter-of-fact way. He entered and closed the door behind him. "I know what Nick likes. How is he?"

Toni's expression turned sad. "He's watching TV in the den. Give me a second; I'll let him know that you're here."

Babocci looked at the pictures on the fireplace mantle: Sonellio's wedding picture and pictures taken at their daughters' graduations. The lamp next to the living room sofa looked familiar. He was examining it when Toni returned. "I've got a lamp just like this—Capodimonte, right?"

"Yes," Toni replied. "It was my parents'. I think it was the only really fine thing they owned."

"Beautiful."

"Thanks. Listen, he's on oxygen. I didn't want you to be shocked."

Babocci pressed his lips together and shook his head sadly. It took him a moment to regroup. "I'll be okay."

"Good." Toni smiled demonstratively to set an example for Babocci and then led him to the den.

"Hey, Jaco," Sonellio said with delight in his voice. "What a nice surprise." He turned to Toni. "Best Italian food on Staten Island."

"I wouldn't know. You never took me there!" Toni said, pretending that she had been offended.

Babocci showed his palms. "Don't be upset, Mrs. Sonellio . . . Café Baci is for gentlemen only."

"Will I be breaking any rules if I have a piece of that tiramisu?"

"*Mi scusi.* Please, help yourself," Babocci said. "Enjoy."

"Coffee, gentlemen?" Toni asked.

"You make espresso in this nice Italian house?" Babocci asked.

"Coming right up." Toni smiled and left the room.

Sonellio hit the pause button—the image of the Starship Enterprise froze on the TV screen. He motioned to the chair next to him, and Babocci sat down. He tugged on the oxygen tube that ran under his nose. "Sorry about this, Jaco. The doctor says I need this right now."

"That don't mean nothing—my aunt, *Zia* Rosalia, wore one of those things for twenty years. My father said she wore it because I cut the cheese too often."

Sonellio chuckled quietly. He had learned to control his laughter so that it didn't hurt quite so much. "And you believed him?"

"I don't know." He shrugged. "I used to fart an awful lot."

Sonellio shook his head in dismay. "You know I haven't asked you in a while, how's your boy?"

Babocci sort of shrugged. "I don't know what to say, Nick. The army took everything from him. He came back from Iraq in pieces. Sometimes I wonder—"

"Don't go there, Jaco," Sonellio warned. "He's a wonderful young man. He'll find his way again."

"I hope so. The poor kid, he'll never have a family of his own. Some Arab motherfucker made sure of that." Babocci sighed deeply. "He's creative."

"Like you?"

"Yeah, although he doesn't enjoy the arts-and-crafts end of it like I do. He likes painting. I guess it's true what they say about the apple not falling far from the tree. You should see the one he's working on now. Nick, I'm not just saying it because he's my kid, but it's fucking gorgeous. I mean it's really something special. I'll ask him if it's okay for you to take a look. He's kind of private about it though. He's down in the basement working on it all day."

"I'm glad to hear he's found something that gives him pleasure."

"It's heartbreaking, ain't it, Nick? He had so much to look forward to. Remember his girlfriend, Luisa? What a stunning kid—*Madonna*. I shouldn't say this, but I got a hard-on every time she walked into the house."

"She's not in the neighborhood anymore?"

"Nah, I don't see her anymore. A beautiful girl like that . . . c'mon, Nick. I'm sure she wanted a family and my poor son . . . like I said, he came back in pieces and unfortunately not all of those pieces work. I mean even if she could look past the arm and leg . . . every girl wants to be a mother. You know what I mean?"

"I'm sorry, Jaco. I really am. Before Toni comes back with the coffee," he leaned forward, "you hear anything?"

Babocci shook his head. "I've got everyone looking: the Cantone boys, Ziggy and Pasquale Millefinucci, everyone I could think of. We monitor the police radio . . . everything. This guy is some kind of lone wolf. No one has heard anything. What about the police, they doing any better?"

"Not really, but Forzo, the assistant chief, has every last man out looking for this monster. Sometimes these investigations take awhile."

"And still nothing? *Madonna.* We're looking for a friggin' ghost."

Toni returned with three portions of tiramisu. "The coffee will be ready in a minute, gentlemen." She turned to walk back to the kitchen but stopped. "I heard the two of you talking. This really gets me angry." She began to cry. "How does someone get away with this? The Jacobys were such nice people."

Sonellio stood and put his arms around her. "We'll get him, sweetheart. No one is going to get away with anything. You have my word."

"That's definite," Babocci said. "This guy is as good as dead. No one does this on *our* turf."

Sonellio gestured to Babocci to tone down the level of his hostility. "One step at a time," he said. "Let's catch the SOB first."

They all jumped when the doorbell rang. "Jesus," Toni said. "Who could that be?" She wiped the tears from her cheek and walked to the front door. She repeated the ritual she carried out whenever the doorbell rang. She moved aside the curtain to take a look outside. She smiled when she saw who was visiting. She pulled the door open. "Stephanie," she said. "What are you doing here?"

~~~

I gave Toni a hug and saw immediately that she had been crying. "How's he doing?"

"He's okay," she said, her voice wavering. "We were just talking about the Jacobys. It's been days, and we haven't heard anything encouraging. That animal is still out on the street."

I hesitated before I spoke. "Can I come in?" I wanted to tell her what I knew, but those words were meant for the boss' ears. "There's been a development."

"Oh dear God." Toni covered her mouth. "Come in, Stephanie. Come in. Nick's friend is here," she said as she led me toward the den. "This is so damn scary. I hope you're bringing Nick good news."

Good news? What exactly defined good news? Yes, we were one step closer to apprehending a murderer, but was I delivering good news? Well, in terms of absolutes, then maybe yes, I was about to deliver good news.

Sonellio pulled the oxygen line from his nose, so that he could give me a hug and a kiss without it getting in the way. "Put that back where it belongs," I said. I had been that route with my father when he was approaching the end and knew that it was not the time for the boss to worry about his vanity. I helped him put the oxygen tube back in place. "How are you feeling, boss?"

Sonellio shrugged. "*Mezzo mezzo*. Stephanie, say hello to a dear friend of mine, Giacomo Babocci."

Babocci was an average-size man. He had thick, white hair and long sideburns. "Stephanie Chalice," I said as I extended my hand.

"Cha-lee-see." He repeated my name phonetically
~~~

separating each syllable. “You’re Frank’s girl?”

“I am. You knew my father?”

“Oh yeah, absolutely. I was sorry to hear about him.” Babocci made the sign of the cross. “God rest his soul. We used to play bocce together back in the old days.”

The idea of my father playing bocce ball made me smile on the inside. I could picture him as a boy, wearing an athletic shirt and shorts, and rolling a bocce ball. “I didn’t know that he—”

“Sure,” Babocci said. “Back in the old days in Brooklyn. You’ve got Frank’s eyes.”

If only that were true. Very few people knew that I was adopted. I had Frank Chalice’s heart and soul, but my eyes . . . they came from someone entirely different. The smile I had been feeling turned into an ache. *God, I miss him so much.* “It’s nice to meet you, Giacomo.”

I spied the dishes of tiramisu set on the coffee table. Toni caught me red-handed. She gave me a pat on the butt. “I’ll bring you some. Giacomo brought it from his restaurant, Café Baci.”

“Baci? That’s Italian for kiss. Café Kiss?”

“Don’t get too excited, Stephanie, it’s for gentlemen only,” Toni said.

“Well,” I huffed, “that certainly let’s all the air out of the romance balloon. Anyway, no arm-twisting necessary—I’d love some. Thanks.” There was so much going on—I actually felt guilty that I had taken a moment to reminisce. I turned back to Sonellio. “I need a word with you,” I said, implying that I needed to speak to him alone.

“About the case?” Sonellio asked. I nodded. “You can talk in front of Giacomo. He’s a neighbor. He’s got a right to know what’s going on.”

“Are you sure?”

Sonellio raised his eyebrows as if to say *are you*

questioning me? Sonellio knew police procedure better than anyone alive. If he said this guy was okay . . . he was okay. I sat down on the couch. Sonellio and Babocci did the same. I knew the first part of what I had to say would be tough for Sonellio to take, but it had to be said nonetheless. "Someone took the four Jacoby bodies." I saw Sonellio's jaw drop. He slumped back against the couch, and his face went white.

"Son of a bitch," Babocci swore. I looked over at him. He was wild-eyed.

"But we know who took them."

Blood slowly flowed back into Sonellio's cheeks. *Thank God.* "What the hell happened, Stephanie?"

"You remember me telling you about Tillerman when I called this morning?"

Sonellio nodded. "The new suspect? Of course. He took them?"

"Ya. He used to work at the Sclafani Funeral Home. He showed up at the ME's office posing as a Sclafani pickup driver and signed for the bodies. He had all the paperwork filled out correctly. Sclafani's a pretty well-known establishment—the ME's office had no reason to question him. A second funeral home came by for the pickup later in the day. That's when all hell broke loose."

"That's fucking unbelievable," Sonellio swore. "What balls!"

"Who the hell is this guy, Tillerman?" Babocci said angrily. "I'll strangle him with my bare hands."

I reached into my jacket pocket and withdrew a freeze frame photo that had been captured on the ME's video security camera. I held it so that both Sonellio and Babocci could see the hulking monster that filled the height and width of the photo. I could see their eyes widen with awe. "You want to strangle this guy? Go ahead, Giacomo. As for me, I'll take a bazooka."

Chapter Forty-four

I was back in the car and on my way to the boat basin near the Verrazano Bridge. I had received a call from Forzo's office, which forced me to leave the Sonellio home almost as soon as I had arrived. God bless Toni—she had smushed my tiramisu into a paper coffee cup, and I was eating it as I drove. I had planned to spend the day looking for Tillerman and interviewing anyone who might have known him, but those plans would have to wait. A body had been spotted in the narrows near the Verrazano Bridge. With any luck, I would arrive just as the body was brought ashore.

I thought about Tillerman as I drove toward the bridge. An all-points bulletin had been issued for his arrest. Tillerman was physically distinctive and could easily be spotted. I hoped that he had not already left the area. I could just see the physical description beneath his photo on a most-wanted poster: huge, monstrously large man with a chest as big as a barrel and arms as thick as fully grown pythons. I mean the guy was a sight to behold. He was conspicuous-looking under any circumstances. Still, I couldn't help wonder how this all tied together. There were the three individual bodies . . . correct that, two bodies and one tablet-shaped medallion, which had presumably been made from the remains of victim number one—how did that tie to the murder of the Jacoby family? The MOs were diametrically discrepant. Presuming that Tillerman was our murderer, he had murdered the first three victims and made medallions from their teeth. He had disposed of victim number one and was about to dispose of victim number three, Vetrov. Only victim number two, Stuart Meisel was found intact. That in itself showed deviation in his MO, which made me uncomfortable. To add further mystery, he had stolen the bodies of the Jacoby family from the ME's office. Serial killers don't normally operate that way. They usually stick to formula and refine their technique as they go along—they deviate from plan only when they encounter an obstacle. Had Tillerman planned to return for the Jacobys? Were their bodies discovered before he had time to retrieve them from their home? I had apples and oranges and was not in the mood for fruit salad.

I saw the towers of the Verrazano Bridge and turned my focus to the newest development. Coast guard ships and police boats were in the water just offshore. Gus was already there, waiting for the body to be carried ashore. I walked over to where he was standing. "And to think I complained about being strapped to my desk—do you believe what's going on here?" The area was a zoo, filled with dozens of police personnel and almost as many police vehicles.

"I always said that you know how to pick 'em," Gus said. "How did it go with the boss?"

"He took it hard but was relieved that we finally have a break in the case. I hope we can wrap this one up quickly."

Gus turned and looked into my eyes. "He's that bad?"

The sun was bright. I reached into my bag and put on my sunglasses. "He's not good. He's on oxygen . . . He looks very weak, Gus. I don't know—" The body was being laid on the embankment just a few yards in front of us. "We'll talk about it later, okay?"

It was a woman's body, and she had been murdered. I knew this because she wore a dress and scuba equipment, a wholly unnatural combination with all the attributes of a diabolical homicide. A scuba tank was attached in the usual manner. A buoyancy control device was fully inflated around her neck. The regulator was still in her mouth and secured with wide, black tape that had been wrapped around her head several times. I was among law enforcement officers who were well accustomed to the sight of a dead body and yet this one touched us all because of the obvious and deliberate nature in which this woman had been killed. It drew a full round of oohs and aahs. The crime scene investigators were on it immediately. Cameras flashed to capture the body in the condition in which it had been discovered.

"This is fucking strange," Gus said. "No scuba mask and she's wearing a dress. First impression?"

"You mean other than she was murdered by a psycho?"

"Uh-huh."

"Only that I can't wait for them to remove the regulator." The victim could have been murdered in several ways, but at the moment none of them were obvious. The opening round of pictures had come to an end. One of the crime scene investigators got on his knees and carefully examined the body for less obvious wounds; small punctures and signs of trauma. It wasn't long afterward that my wait came to an end. He removed the tape and regulator. The woman's gums had been cut and her incisor teeth were gone.

Chapter Forty-five

I sat on the steps outside the medical examiner's office making phone calls and trying to make sense of what I had just heard. The ME's words came back to me. "The subject is an unidentified Caucasian female approximately twenty-one to thirty years of age, whose body was recovered from the narrows not far from the Verrazano Bridge. At the time of rescue, the body was attired in a dress, brassiere, and pantyhose. The victim wore standard scuba equipment suitable for short periods of underwater diving. The equipment recovered with the body included a scuba tank, a buoyancy control device, a weighted diver's belt, a mouth-held air regulator, and pressure gauges. These items have been assigned to the crime lab for study." It takes hours for the ME to do an autopsy—too long for me to sit around waiting.

I heard the door open. I turned and saw Gus standing behind me. "Are you all right?" he asked.

"Life doesn't seem to be worth much around here. That's seven murders, and this guy Tillerman is still at large."

"You know that he won't get very far," Gus said. "We may not know where he is, but we have his picture. How much sneaking around do you think someone the size of the Incredible Hulk can get away with?

"Not a whole hell of a lot. Still, I wish I knew how this all fits together. Why is he killing all these people and why is his MO so inconsistent? It just doesn't make a hell of a lot of sense."

"I know. I hope you're not counting on me for a genius inspiration. I've been racking my brains and haven't come up with anything."

I rubbed Gus' cheek. "If not you, then who?"

He gazed down at my belly. "How about you? Any ideas? Mom and dad could kind of use a little help."

The notion of me giving birth to the world's next great criminal investigator made me smile. "That's an awful lot of pressure to put on someone who's not even toilet-trained. You're not going to be one of those overly demanding fathers, are you?"

Gus smiled. "I'm the easy one. It's you I'm worried about."

"Me?"

"Yes you, Ms. Perfect . . . straight-A student, one of the youngest detectives on the NYPD squad, highest closed-case percentage . . . Do I have to go on?"

"No. It's okay. I get it." I blushed. "And by the way, thank you. Need I remind you that I'm also the girl who went sneaking around with her partner and got *preggers* before saying *I do*. Trust me, I'm capable of tremendous amounts of understanding."

"You only got pregnant because I'm so completely irresistible."

"Yes you are, you Roman God, you." The combination of physical attributes he'd inherited from his Greek mother and Italian father made him classically handsome—he looked like he deserved a place on Mount Olympus. He had all those required features, a square jaw, a Roman nose, and a mop of wavy hair that I just loved to run my fingers through. "Now help me figure out this mess before my contractions start."

"The FBI profilers are stymied," Gus said. "I'm honestly not sure we'll be able to do any better."

"Maybe it's best that we get back to basics—forget the profiling and hit the streets—go house to house, distribute photographs, place ads, and offer rewards."

"I wish I had a better idea," Gus said, "but I don't."

The door opened again. A lab assistant waved to us to come back into the building. "The autopsy is complete," he said. "I think you'll want to hear this." *Oh yes, another coroner's report and more lab results—what could be more stimulating.*

I had been in the conference room so often that I knew which chair had a broken caster—I walked past it to a free roller. Gus began to sit down in the clunker, but I waved him off. We were the first two in the room, but it filled up quickly: Forzo and his executive team, the ME, the chief forensic scientist, and others I had not yet met. It was an ultra high-level case, and Forzo had everyone on it. He looked very unhappy as he awaited the report.

Peter Dambro was the chief medical examiner. He sat down at the conference table and glanced over at Forzo before he spoke. "I'll make this quick. I know that Assistant Chief Forzo and his staff are short on time." Forzo smiled at Dambro and gave him a quick thumbs-up. "A full and detailed report will be available for each of you following the meeting. I have ruled this death a homicide. As you all know, the body of Jane Doe was recovered from the narrows this morning. She was wearing a scuba tank, buoyancy vest, and weight belt. In addition to the obvious mutilation of Jane Doe's jaw and gums, the crime lab has determined that the buoyancy control device was rigged to inflate at a depth of sixty-six feet, when the scuba tank dropped below fifty percent capacity."

Sixty-six feet. *That number is significant.* It took me a moment to recall why that particular depth stood out in my mind. It was the second thing I was taught in scuba class, right after *never leave your buddy.*

Dambro flipped a page in his report, reviewed it, and then began to confer with the chief forensic scientist.

I was sitting next to Detective Sergeant Stanhope, one of Forzo's people. He leaned over and covered his mouth. "Isn't that a lot of trouble to go to just to drown someone?"

"Who said anything about a drowning?"

"What?"

"Just listen." Dambro and the chief forensic scientist had finished conferring. "The other shoe is about to drop."

Dambro cleared his throat. "The victim died as a result of pulmonary barotrauma."

I looked around the table. Forzo understood what Dambro had just said. The others seemed to be confused. Fortunately Gus and I had scuba experience—Gus gave me a knowing glance.

"What does that mean?" Stanhope asked. "How did she die?"

"She surfaced too quickly. Her lungs exploded."

Chapter Forty-six

Ambler showed up just as the medical examiner's meeting broke up. He grabbed us and sat us down for a quick briefing. "I'm crazed," Ambler said. "I was sitting on the goddamn Gowanus Expressway forever—two hours for a one-hour ride."

Ambler was solo. "You should have asked Agent Banks along for company—the ride wouldn't have seemed so long."

Ambler raised his pointer finger. "Not now, Chalice. Jesus, I hate Staten Island."

"Why? What's wrong with Staten Island?"

"I'll tell you what's wrong," he said in a huff. "It's not Manhattan! Now tell me what I missed." Ambler poured himself a glass of water and sat down. His face was flush, and he was sweating through his suit jacket.

"A woman's body was found this morning, floating in the narrows," Gus said.

"I've heard the basics, Gus. Just give me the forensic details," Ambler said.

"The victim's incisors were cut out, just as in the three previous cases," Gus added.

"I got that too." Ambler was not in the best mood.

"The victim was outfitted with scuba gear," I said. "a tank and regulator, weight belt, and a buoyancy control device, which had been tampered with to inflate at a depth of sixty-six feet when the tank was half empty."

Ambler was no slouch. He knew where this was going already. "Triggering rapid-ascent decompression trauma."

"Correct. The water in the narrows is between seventy and ninety feet deep. Tillerman knew the depth of the water and set the BCD to inflate at a pressure of two atmospheres." I pictured this poor woman in the icy water at the bottom of the Staten Island Narrows with her eyes closed, waiting for her air to run out. I didn't know why Tillerman had selected this victim, but he had chosen a particularly heinous way to kill her. Scuba divers breathe in pressurized air from an air tank. Atmospheric pressure doubles with every thirty-three feet of depth. Everything works out okay as long as the diver surfaces slowly, taking sufficient time to depressurize on the way up. Jane Doe would have rocketed to the surface when her buoyancy control device inflated. Water pressure against her body dropped suddenly, and the gases in her lungs expanded explosively. Her lungs popped like a balloon.

"What's the water temperature down there?" Ambler asked.

"Cold as hell."

"That's what I'm thinking," Ambler said, "She had to be hypothermic by the time the BCD inflated."

"I don't know how long it would have taken for her heart to stop. Until we hear differently, we'll have to stick with the ME's conclusion and that she was still alive when she surfaced."

"There was no way for this woman to make a controlled ascent to the surface before the BCD inflated?" Ambler asked.

"The ME noted severe swelling in the area of the second cervical vertebrae, which he felt was the result of a compression injury. She was also bound around the wrists and ankles."

"So Tillerman whacked her over the head before he

threw her into the narrows. Temporary paralysis?"

"That's what the ME suspects," Gus said. "The big Russian's neck was snapped as well—it goes to his MO."

"So we have another murder, and I suppose another medallion will be delivered to FBI headquarters shortly," Ambler said.

"The victim's incisors were removed postmortem," Gus added. "The SOB waited for the body to surface to cut her teeth out. He put the regulator back in her mouth and reapplied tape."

"Why?" Ambler snapped. "Why go to the trouble?"

"Isn't it obvious?"

"No, Chalice, it's not," Ambler retorted. "Explain."

"He was afraid that she'd choke on blood if he cut out her teeth while she was still alive and that's not how he wanted her to die. His method is so specific. He thought it through well in advance."

"Then he replaces the regulator and tapes it again?" Ambler asked. "Why?"

"Because he was being a good little psycho—he didn't want the body to fill with sea water. He preserved the evidence. He's helping us with our case."

Chapter Forty-seven

Fallujah, Iraq, November 24, 2004: Eight hours before Thanksgiving.

PFC Tom Babocci dove for cover. He buried his face in the sand when he heard the whistle he knew preceded a mortar explosion. He was thirty meters from the blast, barely beyond the effective blast radius of the 60mm Iraqi mortar round. Despite being out of range, he could feel the pressure waves from the explosion pummel his body. Sand sprayed his face with such intensity that grains became embedded in his skin. He remained motionless for a moment, despite knowing that he was a sitting duck should another mortar round drop nearby. He could feel his heart pound forcefully within his chest. He thanked God for sparing his life. It took another moment before he could will his body to move.

An M35 cargo truck had fallen to enemy fire. The remains of the overturned transport seemed to him like a good spot to take shelter from the sun and the wind. Babocci scrambled over to the metal skeleton and drank from his canteen. The water was warm and unappealing. He had filled his canteen from a PVC storage tank that was left out in the sun—it had imparted a miserable taste to the unfiltered water. The troops were warned about the perils of dehydration on a daily basis. He drank as much as he could stand.

Another mortar round exploded much farther away than the last. A third round landed still further west. The Iraqi attack was moving away from him, providing a momentary opportunity for him to catch his breath. He sat for several minutes looking out at the vast and unremarkable desert. Before him, shades of tan and sienna played in the wind, exchanging colors and mixing to become one. *Oh, how I'd love to see something green, a bush, a weed . . . anything.* He found the monotony of the desert depressing. It was almost as bad as the solitude. His troop would be along soon to pick him up, but until then . . .

He kept her picture with him always. Looking at Luisa's picture, he could not remember a time when he did not love her. He had fallen for her before they had ever exchanged a word. He had admired her in school and in the neighborhood and had noted every detail of her appearance: her silky, long, black hair and her slender waist, the profile of her nose, and her long eyelashes . . . the reserved exchanges they shared. *Thank God she noticed me.* He was fatally bashful, and they would have never spoken had Luisa not made the first move. It was easy after that, easy and natural. They were meant for each other.

He ached when he saw her picture, knowing she would not be in his arms for another year. "I can't wait for you to come back to me," she said the last time they spoke. The wait was torturous. She was on his mind every conscious second of the day.

A gust of wind kicked up unexpectedly. The rusted truck creaked. Sand blew into his mouth. He spit out as much as he could and then rinsed his mouth with more foul water. He wiped his mouth and took a deep breath of the arid Iraqi air. All was quiet for a moment. He allowed the silence to calm him. His mind was just beginning to settle down when he heard a cry for help. It was coming from somewhere nearby. Babocci got to his feet and cautiously took a look around. He walked around the truck and saw the remains of a few ramshackle homes in the distance. "Help." He heard the voice again, a soft plea that disappeared behind the rushing wind. "Is someone there?" It was not an American's voice. He paused for a moment while he considered the possibility of stumbling into an enemy trap. He scanned the landscape and then his focus returned to the bombed-out homes in front of him. "Please. Someone help us, please."

The troop will be along soon. Better to wait.

He heard a woman's voice crying out in anguish. "Dear God, save us." He ventured closer. The cries for help had stopped for a moment. As he got closer, he could hear the muted sound of Hebrew prayers.

All that was left of the decimated home were shattered walls and a few cooking pots. The house had a sand floor. The wind whipped up again. The sand near his feet swirled, and he saw that it covered wooden boards. He heard the wood boards creaking beneath his boots. "Help us!" Voices came to life beneath him, crying for help. "Our prayers have been answered. Dear God thank you. Are you American?"

Babocci was silent for a moment while he considered his next move. He brushed the sand on the floor with his boot until he found the outline of the cellar door. The hasp that held the door closed was secured with a rusted metal bolt. He kicked the bolt free, stepped back, and aimed his rifle at the door. "Come on out," he said. He waited for someone to emerge. The door lifted slowly. A small child was visible in the opening. Babocci looked into the cellar and saw that the little girl was standing on a man's shoulders. The man was dressed in civilian clothing. Babocci lowered his rifle and then slung it over his shoulder. He reached down and lifted the child up out of the cellar. As he did, he could see that the man was crying. "It's all right," Babocci said. "I'm American."

"God bless you," the man said. He bent down and lifted a second small girl toward the opening.

The family that Babocci rescued was standing around him and crying with relief. "I am Rabbi Asa Borach. I don't know how to thank you—you saved my family." He stepped forward and hugged Babocci. His wife did the same. "What is your name, soldier? I want to say a prayer in your honor."

"PFC Tom Babocci. How long have you been down there?"

"Almost three days. Do you have any water? The children . . . please if you can spare a sip."

Babocci handed him the canteen. "It's not very good."

Borach unscrewed the cap and held the canteen while the smallest girl drank. "Not too much," he said. "Just take what you need."

"Finish it," Babocci said. "My troop will be along soon."

Borach waited for his second daughter and wife to drink before he took any water for himself. "Thank you," he said. "This is the best water I have ever tasted."

"You're working with Israeli intelligence?" Babocci asked.

Borach nodded. "We are on the same team."

"Until the Iraqis discovered your true identity. I'm surprised you weren't shot immediately."

"The Iraqis left us down there with no food and water. They wanted me to watch my children wither and die. A bullet would have been more humane."

~~~

Babocci lifted Borach's youngest daughter and placed her in the U.S. Army transport vehicle. The
~~~

transport was full—there was barely room for the small child to squeeze in between her parents. She threw her arms around him and kissed him on the cheek. "Thank you," she whispered in her small voice.

The transport driver slapped Babocci on the shoulder. "You okay here until the rest of the troop comes by? Shouldn't be too long."

Babocci nodded. He was still looking at the little girl and marveling at the way a child can warm your heart. "Yeah, I refilled my canteen. I'll be all right."

"You're a good man, Tommy," the transport driver said. "These rabbis risk their lives for us. This one would have become a martyr if you hadn't found them." He reached into his shirt pocket and handed Babocci a pack of gum. "Here, enjoy. I'll see you back at camp."

Rabbi Borach and his family were still waving to Babocci as the transport disappeared into the distance.

Babocci continued to look out at the horizon long after the transport was gone. He was reaching for his canteen when a sniper round hit him in the chest. The velocity of the bullet knocked him to the ground. He was still dazed when the Iraqi sniper raced over to him and leveled his rifle to finish the job.

Chapter Forty-eight

US Military Hospital, Balad, Iraq, November 30, 2004.

Major General Randolph Clemmens, the head of Joint Special Operations Command, followed Brigadier General Ralph Totem through the hospital complex on their way to the pulmonary care unit. Totem stopped dead in his tracks as soon as he hit the area. "Here it is. See for yourself," Totem said. "Every bed is full. I've got others spread out all around the hospital."

Clemmens rubbed his chin. "Look, Ralph, are you absolutely sure that all of these cases are coming from the burn pits?"

"With all due respect, General, we use an area the size of a football field to burn waste for a thirty-thousand-soldier military base. We're using jet fuel to burn plastics, truck batteries, chemicals, tires, munitions, mess hall waste, and every other possible kind of garbage imaginable in an open-air pit. What did you think was going to happen?"

"Are you sure that some of them aren't malingerers? You know how it goes. Every goldbrick knows how to play the game. They hear how a couple of troops got sick, and they jump on the bandwagon."

"Malingerers? No, they're not malingerers. If you like, I can take a few of them off their oxygen and you can listen to them wheeze."

"You're out of line, Ralph. You see me standing here. I know that you're serious."

"Randy, I've been petitioning to close the burn pits since the day I got here. You're exposing tens of thousands of military personnel to dangerous airborne toxins every day. The troops have asthma, emphysema, and COPD. Stick around and watch. The sky fills with black acrid smoke, and we're all breathing it in . . . including me!"

"And I've been trying to allocate the funds to replace them, but it hasn't been easy. We have eighty goddamn burn pits in operation throughout the Middle East, and it will cost millions to replace them with high-temperature incinerators."

"What do you think it will cost when the class action lawsuits start rolling in? These kids are over here risking their lives. They have to survive enemy attack day after day. They're lucky enough if they make it out of the desert alive. It's not right that their own government puts them at risk over something like this. I don't give a shit that these burn pits are operated by giant defense contractors with half of the US Senate in their pockets. This-has-got-to-stop."

Clemmens came face to face with Totem, his eyes were red with anger. "I-have-got-the-message. Now unless you're ready to be relieved of your command—"

"I've had enough. I'm putting in for a transfer," Totem said.

"And I'll approve it. I'm doing the best I can." A tense moment passed. "I want to see the boys that have been injured in the field." Clemmens walked off. He came upon Babocci's bed. Babocci was unconscious and on life support. His amputated arm and leg stumps were visible for Clemmens to see. "What happened to this soldier?"

Totem still looked angry as he read Babocci's chart. "PFC Tommaso Babocci—I heard about this one. He took a sniper round in the chest. He had just rescued an Israeli family who had been imprisoned by the Iraqis."

"Israeli intelligence?"

"Ya, the Mossad plants families behind enemy lines. They act to inform the US military and keep the opposition from taking root."

"This man is a hero. I'll see that he's decorated for his valor."

I'm sure he'd rather have his limbs back. Don't say that, Ralph. Keep your mouth shut.

"You said he took a round in the chest. What happened to his arm and leg?"

"The sniper was a real motherfucker. Babocci was alone. He came back and made chop meat out of his arm, leg, and genitals." Clemmens winced. "We had no choice but to amputate. He's lucky to be alive. We're keeping him under heavy sedation until he gets stronger. He's still critical."

Clemmens covered his mouth and was silent for moments. He leaned over and stroked Babocci's hair. "I'm sorry this happened to you, son. I'm truly sorry."

"He took eighteen rounds, one in the chest and seventeen in his left arm and leg. He was conscious when his troop picked him up."

"Eighteen? Why eighteen? The Iraqis use Russian Tabuks, don't they?"

"That's right, Randy, they do."

"Well, don't the Tabuk magazines hold twenty rounds? I can't believe the son of a bitch didn't empty the clip."

"That's right, the clip holds twenty," Totem said. "Every Arab knows that eighteen is the Jewish number for good luck."

Chapter Forty-nine

Gus and I stopped for a dinner break. We found this enormous diner on Highland Boulevard. Now diners aren't normally my thing, but this one was a real find. The service was quick, the food was fresh, and the portions were large enough to choke a horse . . . or a ravenous pregnant woman. The diner looked like it had recently been redecorated. My maternity-heightened senses were still hard at work. I took a whiff and determined that the vinyl the booth was upholstered with was brand spanking new.

The place was packed. I wasn't surprised. The prices were dirt cheap. My tuna melt came with an avalanche of toasty golden onion rings. Onion rings are like heroin to me—deep-fried, batter-coated heroin. "Want some?" Gus reached for one but I blocked him with my hand. "I think it's only fair to warn you that I'm hoarding these." Gus snatched one and smirked while he chewed it. I picked up a butter knife. "I wouldn't try that again if I were you!"

The guy sitting across the way from us was bald but had a huge wad of hair growing out of his ear. He slurped his soup so loudly I wanted to hand him a straw. "Jesus," I said to Gus. "Please, put me out of my misery."

"Relax, it's only a cup of soup—he's almost done."

I glanced over at his cup of soup and did a quick calculation. "He's got about ten spoonfuls left. I'll never make it."

Gus held my hand and pretended to be serious. "You

can do it. Stay with me, Stephanie. I'll talk you through it."

Our tableside guest did it again—he emitted a slurp so loud that the window shades rattled. "I can't take it, I tell you. I've become intolerant of bad manners."

"Easy girl."

I reached into my bag and found my Etymotic shooters plugs. I stuffed them in my ears.

"Now that's ridiculous," Gus said.

"What?"

"I said *that's ridiculous.*"

"I still can't hear you." I started to giggle. The waitress came over with two plates of baklava. I removed the earplugs. Her name badge read Cathy. "Are those for us, Cathy?"

"On the house," she said." "She leaned over the table. "It's the least I can do. Old Stavros over there slurps so loudly it makes me feel like I'm at the dentist's office. You know, when they stick the suction tube in your mouth so that you don't drool on yourself."

I glared at Gus. "See, I told you it was bad." Cathy put the dishes down in front of us. "Gee, this looks awesome. Thanks."

"You're cops, right?" Cathy asked.

"It's that obvious?" Gus said.

Cathy nodded. "Can I ask you a question? What the hell is going on around here? I read all the papers. Staten Island is starting to sound like Fort Apache. There are bodies turning up all over the place . . . another one this morning, floating in the narrows, right?"

I nodded as I took a forkful of baklava. "I won't lie to you, it's not good, but I think we're getting close. Oh wow, this is delicious."

"We do all the baking on premises," Cathy said. "So

you're looking for this guy Tillerman, right?"

"That's right." I sensed that Cathy had something to tell us, and that perhaps her need to chat was the real reason for the free dessert. "You want to sit down?"

Cathy looked toward the front counter, presumably to see if her boss was watching. "Okay, only for a moment. Scoot over." I made room for Cathy but took my dessert with me. I can eat and listen at the same time—I'm a magnificent multitasker. "I used to live on Arden Avenue. I knew his wife, Barbara. We used to volunteer at the JCC soup kitchen on Manor Road."

"Did you ever meet him?" Gus asked.

"Sure. Big guy. Didn't talk much though. They have two adorable little boys, Mark and Stephen."

"How long ago was that?"

Cathy shrugged. "I don't know . . . several months, a year maybe?"

"So what happened?"

"She stopped coming down to the JCC. The next thing I knew they were boarding up the house. Times are hard—I figured they couldn't afford the upkeep on the house. I guess the bank owns it now."

"Actually the house used to belong to his parents. He took it over. There's no mortgage. He's in arrears on the taxes, but you know how quickly the county moves," I said facetiously. "I'm afraid that house will be an eyesore for a long time to come. It was boarded up to keep out looters."

"Too bad," Cathy said. "Barbara kept a loving home."

"So you never stayed in touch?" Gus asked.

"No," Cathy said. "I feel guilty about it because Barbara was such a lovely woman. I hope she's all right. I can't believe her husband is a murderer."

"Actually, Cathy, he's only a suspect at this moment, but I know what you mean," Gus said. "I guess you just never know."

"Well, thanks for the dessert." It seemed as if Cathy was just being nosey and didn't have anything else to contribute to our investigation. I handed her my business card. "Call me if you think of anything that might help."

Cathy got up just as my cell phone rang. "Good luck, detectives. I hope you catch him soon."

"Another medallion," Ambler said over the phone. "The forensic odontologist has already examined the teeth which were used to make the medallion and compared them to the impressions he took from the mouth of the woman found in the narrows this morning—he believes they came from her mouth."

"I'd be surprised if they didn't. Was this one delivered in the same way?"

"Yeah. Someone paid a kid to drop it off in the lobby," Ambler said.

"Same useless description?"

"Yeah, an average-size white guy in a hoodie and sunglasses," Ambler said. "Gave him twenty bucks to walk the envelope across town to the FBI building."

"And no fingerprints?"

"Clean as a whistle," Ambler replied.

"So whomever is handing off these packages is not Tillerman. I think it's fair to say that Tillerman is not an average-size white guy. Besides, there's no way he'd take a chance on being seen in the vicinity of your office, not a gargantuan hulking character like that."

"So who's his accomplice?" Ambler asked.

"And that's one to grow on."

"Thanks, Chalice you're a big help," Ambler said. "Later." I disconnected.

Gus had a puzzled expression on his face. "And that's one to grow on? Where in God's name did that come from?"

"Oh come on, Gus, they used to play that public service announcement in between the Saturday morning cartoons. You don't remember?"

"I guess now that you mention it." Gus smiled after a moment. "God love ya, you're strange."

I patted the back of Gus' hand. "Buckle up, baby, there's more to come."

Okay, so there was someone else in the picture, a delivery boy if nothing else. The new information did not get me excited. I knew that we had to find Tillerman before he struck again. The burning question was why had Tillerman gone to such great lengths to kill Jane Doe. She was his first female victim and that was also a deviation from his MO. It did not explain why he had devised such a devious method to kill her. I drummed my fingers on the table. "It's right there, Gus. I feel like I should get it, but I don't."

"You'll figure it out. I have faith in you."

I pushed my dessert plate to the center of the table. "I can't eat anymore."

Gus' mouth dropped. "For real?"

"Yes, for real. And don't bother asking; I feel all right."

Chapter Fifty

Giacomo Babocci zipped his leather jacket and looked in the mirror to check his hair. He began to turn gray before he was thirty, but his hair was still dense and lustrous. He smoothed the hair on the side of his head with an open palm. *You've got a few more wrinkles since Angela died . . . but your hair still looks good.* His wife's picture hung on the wall nearby. He kissed it. "I still love you, babe."

He opened the door that led to the basement and hustled down the stairs. The house was a large ranch with a full basement. It was built in the fifties by Italian tradesmen and Babocci often boasted that it was built so solidly it could withstand a nuclear attack. "Hey, Tommy, I'm going out." His deep voice echoed through the cavernous basement. "Hey, Tommy, you down here?" He heard the toilet flush and turned toward the bathroom. He could see his son through the partially opened door. He adjusted his focus so that it was off his son and on the wall-mounted shelf that contained boxes of disposable catheters, sterile lubricant, and toilet paper. He ached for his son whenever he saw his supplies. *They say the army turns boys into men—not this time. Thank God he can do that on his own now.* Inserting the catheter with one hand was difficult and there were many times when Giacomo needed to assist him when he first came home from the VA hospital.

He waited for the noise of the flushing toilet to subside. It took an additional moment for him to gain control of his emotions. He wiped some moisture from the corner of his eye. “Hey, Tommy, you almost done? I’m going out.”

Tom opened the bathroom door with his prosthetic hand. He smiled at his father while he cinched his belt. “Where are you heading, dad? It’s almost your bedtime.”

“Don’t be a wise guy. I’ve got business.”

“Business? What kind of business? Baci is closed for the night.”

“Shitty business. It’s this Jacoby thing. The police have a suspect.”

“They found the guy who murdered that family?”

“No, they didn’t find him; they’re looking for him. The boys and me are trying to help. I’ve got every *paesano* I know out looking for this sonofabitch.”

“And you think you’ll find him before the police do?”

“Hey, we may be a bunch of old guineas, but we know our shit. We’ve been taking care of our own for many, many years. Don’t be surprised if this guy ends up in the river before the police get their hands on him. You think I want this guy in the jerk-off court system wasting everyone’s time for the next five years? I don’t think so. Sometimes street justice is best.”

“Can I help?”

Babocci put his hands on his son’s shoulder and smiled. “How would you like to help?”

“You know I did recon in the army. I know how to find people.”

“Sure. Why not? You want to help; let’s go. I want this son of a bitch found before my friend Nick is no longer of this world.”

“Nick, that’s the old chief of detectives, right? I remember him. Nice man.”

“Nice man? He’s a fucking saint. I’d lie down my life for him. I know him almost forty years.”

"He's sick?"

"Dying of cancer. It's terrible. I went over to his place before. He looks like hell." Babocci shook his head sadly and then turned to inspect the large glass painting Tom had been working on. "How's the masterpiece coming along?"

"It's done, dad." I finished it yesterday."

Babocci took a few steps closer so that he could better see the details of his son's work. "That's gorgeous, Tommy. I'm very proud of you." He noticed another piece of glass, comparable in size to the one that had just been completed. "I see you're ready to start a new one." Tom shook his head excitedly. "Beautiful." He gave his son a kiss on the cheek. "Grab your jacket if you're serious about helping. I'm sure the boys would love to see you."

"Okay. You don't mind?"

"Mind? It's like the passing of the torch. I've been part of this neighborhood over sixty years. No one comes in here and does what that piece of shit did to the Jacobys. No one!"

Chapter Fifty-one

It was first light when I pulled up in front of Michael Tillerman's abandoned home. Gus and I agreed to split up for a while so that we could cover more ground. The APB on Tillerman was more than forty-eight hours old, and we had yet to receive a single worthwhile tip. Forzo had the entire Staten Island Police Department on high alert for our suspect. The fact that he hadn't been found probably meant that he was hunkered down somewhere and not moving around. He would have to surface at some point—it was a waiting game I didn't have the patience to play.

I thought I would be the first one on the scene at Tillerman's, but I was wrong. A vintage BMW 2002tii was parked in front of the house. I recognized the car—Damien Zugg was already inside.

Zugg was on the floor in the kitchen, trying to grab something that must have fallen between the cabinets and the wall. He was like a forensic Hoover trying to suck up clues.

"Shit," he said. He pushed away from the corner of the cabinet and stood up. He turned around and smiled at me.

"What did you find down there?"

He was holding a small object with long-nose tweezers. "I thought I found a slug back there, but it's just a Raisinet," he said as he dropped it into the kitchen sink.

"You're up early. I thought I'd find this place

deserted."

"I didn't sleep well," Zugg said. "I got up and went through my personal email. Did you know that Columbian women are nearby and waiting to hear from me?"

"That's news."

"I know and that's not all—Russian brides and hot Asian chicks are chomping at the bit to be with me, which makes sense because I also learned that I can get Viagra without a prescription. They're available twenty-four hours a day."

I snickered.

"What's a MILF?"

Oh dear Lord. I was a little embarrassed but I figured hey, we're all adults here. "It stands for mothers I'd like to . . . fill in the ending."

Zugg looked embarrassed. "Sorry, I guess I could have looked it up on my own."

"No worries. I received an email from Swaziland this morning. I'm getting an inheritance of twelve million dollars. Imagine my surprise to learn that I had relatives in Africa. It's a very serendipitous morning for both of us." Zugg grinned. "Now that we've discussed our good fortunes . . . find anything other than the Raisinet?"

"Except for the basement, the house looks as if it has been unoccupied for a long time. The Tillerman's must have moved out in a hurry because most of the family possessions seem to have been left behind."

"Middle of the night kind of thing?"

"That's my thinking as well: clothing, furniture, toys—they're all still here," Zugg said.

"Furniture is one thing, but if you were moving with your kids, wouldn't you at least take a few of their favorite things? I mean even if you're in a hurry—"

"Oh I agree. We now know that Michael Tillerman

has a wife and two young boys. Their baseball gloves are still in the upstairs bedroom. I saw a Nintendo 3DS up there too—small items . . . certainly you'd take them to keep the boys entertained. I mean even if you were whisking them away in the middle of the night . . . maybe his wife took the kids and left him, or maybe—"

"They're dead," I met Zugg's glance—we both seemed to be on the same page. "There are no records on any member of the Tillerman family in the past year. It's as if they fell off the face of the earth. He could have killed them himself. I was confused as to why Tillerman has a necropsy table and embalming supplies in his basement. It doesn't match his MO, but his own family . . . could it be that he murdered them?"

"And did what with the bodies?" Zugg asked.

"Buried them? Disposed of them? Who knows? He had the skill and equipment to do it. Maybe he killed them and then gave them a proper funeral. I mean the man is a certifiable lunatic, isn't he? I'm still stymied by the extreme method he used to kill the woman in the narrows. He dropped her in the water and brought her up so quickly that her lungs exploded. I mean, come on, that's so specific. Why would he do it that way?" I shrugged. "I'm not doing anyone any good flapping my gums. I'm going to have another look around."

I walked into the dining room, which was decorated very simply. The walls were painted light green. The table, chairs, and side table were dark mahogany. The furniture looked pretty dated. I remembered that Tillerman had inherited the home from his parents—the dining room set was probably theirs. A vase was set in the middle of the side table. As with everything else, the vase had simply been left behind with flowers in it. The water had evaporated and the flowers had long ago withered and dried over the top of the vase. The pieces began to fit into place. It was difficult to recognize the vase with the dried white petals stuck to it, but the longer I stared at it the more it began to look familiar. I hovered over the vase, staring down at it. I tried to connect the dots. "Hey, Damien, can you come in here for a minute?"

Zugg didn't answer but I heard footsteps and saw him walk into the room a moment later. "Yes?"

I pointed to the side table. "That vase, there's something familiar about it. I just can't put my finger on it."

The vase was modern in style with sharply angled ridges. Zugg picked it up and examined it. It wasn't until he lifted it up, overhead, that I was able to see the pattern on the base. It had six sharp points and six sharp grooves. The base made up a six-pointed star.

Zugg confirmed a moment later. "It's a hexagram."

"Damien, do you know what kind of flowers those are?"

The petals were difficult to make out. They had dried against the glass and decomposed to the point of being semi-transparent. Zugg studied them for a moment. "I believe they're lilies. Polygonatum multiflorum perhaps."

"I can barely see them, and you've narrowed it down to an exact genus and species? You're pretty amazing, Damien. I saw a vase like that before, but I can't remember where. Is that a common variety of lily?"

"You see them outdoors more than you might see them in an indoor floral arrangement—the petals are pretty small. There's a more common name for them. They're called Solomon's Seal."

It wasn't until Zugg said *Solomon's Seal* that I realized why the vase looked so familiar. "I saw an identical vase, and it was also filled with small lilies. It was on the side table near the staircase in the Jacoby house.

“Solomon’s Seal is also the name for a six-sided star or the Star of David.” The pieces were beginning to fit together. Zugg had a deadly serious expression on his face.

“Are you thinking what I’m thinking?”

“Yes,” Zugg said. “Whoever killed the Jacobys may have killed the Tillermans as well.”

Chapter Fifty-two

Michael Tillerman sat in a Buick Century waiting for 5:00 a.m. to arrive. He had stashed the panel van, knowing that the police would be looking for the vehicle he had used for the pickup from the ME's office.

His right hand was locked in spasm and had been since he'd dug the grave in the middle of the night. He tried to flex his paralyzed hand, but it remained rigid.

He reached into his pocket with his left hand and pulled out a handful of tablets. *Eight*, he decided. It was the most he'd ever taken. He counted out the Repressor tablets and swallowed them down with a gulp of water. *Today's the day.* He began to think about what lay in store for him. His heart began to pound from a powerful surge of adrenaline. It pounded with such force that Tillerman could feel the seatback rock from the force of each beat. He tried the Valsalva maneuver, to reduce the force of the palpitations. He closed his mouth, pinched his nostrils, and blew until his eardrums began to ache, but it did not relieve the fierce palpitations. He tried the exact opposite, taking several deep, rhythmic breaths in an effort to calm down. He broke out in an abrupt, drenching sweat. He opened the windows hoping fresh air might help. His cell phone vibrated. It took his mind off the palpitations. "Hello?"

"It's time. Come around the back."

Tillerman checked his watch. Somehow 5:00 a.m. had come and gone while he attempted triage. *Dear God, it's time.* He began to shake uncontrollably. He had experienced severe tremors and spasm before, which he assumed were side effects of his medication, but this time he was sure that his symptoms were due to nerves.

It was still dark when he left the car, which he had parked on a secluded dead-end street. He walked quickly through the greenbelt until it would take him no further. He had lived on Staten Island all of his life and knew the undeveloped land from memory—he had often played there as a child and could still remember some of the landmarks that had endured since his youth. When he left the greenbelt, he cut through backyards and school grounds until he arrived at his destination and went inside.

He waited for Tillerman in the shadows as he always did. He wore a pure white, hooded cloak that hid his face from Tillerman's sight. He kept his face down while he spoke. "You have completed the four sacrifices as required. Are you ready?"

Tillerman breathed nervously. He nodded. "Yes. I'm ready."

He held out a folded white cloak. It was the same as the one he was wearing. He said a prayer in an Aramaic tongue to bless the cloak before he handed it to Tillerman. "Change into this. Wear nothing else." He pointed to a bathroom. "I'll wait for you here."

Tillerman took the white cloak and walked into the bathroom. He emerged a few minutes later and saw that the floor was covered with a large printed cloth, which bore the pattern of a six-sided star.

"Sit in the center of the star. Sit within the Seal of Solomon."

Tillerman took a few delicate steps in his bare feet so as not to disturb the cloth. He sat down in the center of the seal, facing four copper urns. Each bore the same six-sided marking.

"Are you ready?"

Tillerman closed his eyes for a moment while he drew strength from within and to find inner peace. He nodded to proceed.

He sang in the Aramaic language, chanting what Tillerman perceived to be a prayer. "You have delivered a sacrifice for each of the elements of life. Before you are the four vessels of Solomon. You must consume the contents of each." He knelt beside Tillerman and removed the seal from the first urn. He poured brown powder from the first urn into Tillerman's cupped hand. "This symbolized the earth. It must be breathed through the nostrils."

Tillerman looked down at the substance in his palm and snorted the full amount into his nose without hesitation. It took a few moments for the burning in his nostrils to subside. His vision began to blur almost immediately. He could feel his eyelids become heavy as a veil descended over him.

"What's going on?" Tillerman asked. "I feel so—"

He placed a finger to his lips. "You are being prepared for your voyage. You're almost ready." He picked up the second urn and removed the seal right under Tillerman's nose. A white vapor drifted upward from the opening. "Breathe it in, Michael. Breathe in the air." Tillerman inhaled the vapor. It had a pungent character but did not burn his nostrils as the previous substance had.

"Am I ready now?" Tillerman asked.

"Almost." He removed the seal from the third urn and held a lit candle to the opening. A small blue flame ignited at the top of the bottle. He offered the urn to Tillerman. "Now drink in the fire."

Tillerman felt his concentration ebbing. It took a moment before he was able to focus on the opening of the bottle.

"Drink, Michael." He lifted the back of the urn until the fiery liquid rushed into Tillerman's mouth. He held it in place while Tillerman gulped it all down. He smiled as Tillerman coughed from the irritating liquid. "Only one element to go. You're doing so well." He removed the seal from the last urn and handed it to Tillerman. "This is the easiest one. Here, a simple sip of water and it is done."

Tillerman's entire body shook. He seized the last urn and chugged the water. He was barely able to force the last of it down.

"You did very well, Michael." He held out a candle for Tillerman to take in his hands. "Now pray, Michael. Pray for your family's return." He covered Tillerman's head with the white hood. "Close your eyes and pray."

Tillerman could barely make out the image within the shadowy recesses of the large hood. He gave up after a moment and closed his eyes. He heard footsteps and then the sound of the cellar door closing. His mind began to drift. He saw an image in his mind, but it was too distorted for him to recognize. Before him, light began to twist and bend. The room turned into a prism of brilliantly colored lights. He heard his sons calling to him. He could hear their small voices growing louder and louder. The ocean came into view in the distance. His old house stood at the water's edge. He grinned as his sons' faces came into view. They were smiling as they ran to him across the grassy lawn. He could feel his heart swelling with happiness as he reached out for them. His fingertips tingled in anticipation of caressing them. They were almost in his arms when everything went black.

Chapter Fifty-three

I was reviewing a lab report when the handsome Dr. Nigel Twain entered the conference room. He pulled off his jacket and crossed the room to greet me. I got out of my chair and stood up to welcome him. His new diet and exercise regimen had paid dividends—his arms felt rock hard as I hugged him. He was wearing an intoxicating cologne. I think the fragrance is called *Tear My Clothes Off.* Okay so that's not the actual name, but that was the first thought to cross my mind. Yes, I'm a good girl, but sometimes it's fun to play with the notion of being bad. I guess that's the sort of thing that makes us human. He stepped back to take a better look at me. "You look wonderful," he said.

That's it, compliment me, play havoc with my libido. As if I didn't feel wicked enough. His words were like accelerant, and I was the flame. Thank God my love for Gus was stronger than my lust for Twain. I always wondered if he knew how strong an effect he had on me. Was he toying with me? There was a time before Gus and I were together when Twain had declared his interest for me. He had been quite forward at the time. I was never really sure if his comments were intentional or coincidental, but by God, I didn't want them to stop. I tried to shame myself into switching gears. I pictured a YouTube video in which a well-endowed pregnant woman tore the clothes off a hunky dark guy. How scandalous? How shocking? How completely Stephanie Chalice. *Reset the thermostat*, I told myself. *Get back to work.*

"Thanks, Nigel, it's only been a week—what did you expect to see, a blob of a woman in threadbare stretch pants?"

Twain snickered. "No, I didn't expect that at all. It's just that—"

"I know. I'm getting bigger."

"Exactly, love, and no need to worry—you're every inch the vivacious beauty you've always been."

Jesus, he's killing me. "Thanks, and thanks for taking the time to run across the bridge to meet with me."

"Never a problem, love. The Jaguar needed some badly needed exercise anyway. I haven't had it out in ages."

Twain drove a gorgeous supercharged XJ-R. More importantly, I loved the way he pronounced Jaguar *(Jag-yu-warr).* I could listen to Twain's deep English baritone for days. Okay, maybe not days—at some point the idea of ripping his clothes off would surface again. *Oh dear.* "Got time for a little shop talk?"

"That's why I'm here. Fire away. More questions about that family that was murdered in Staten Island?"

"Maybe."

"Maybe?"

"The Jacoby case seems to be related to another string of murders I've been investigating. I feel pretty sure that the same guy is involved in both."

"Sounds complicated."

"Aren't they always?" We both sat down at the conference table. "Let me know what you make of this. Separate and apart from the Jacoby case, there were four murders that the FBI brought me in to help with. After each murder, a tablet-shaped medallion was recovered."

"Tablet-shaped?"

"Like the tablet Moses used to inscribe the Ten Commandments, a rectangle rounded on one side."

"Intriguing. Go on."

Twain has a strong religious background. He's deeply interested in religious history and the effects that religion has on the workings of the human mind. As I mentioned before, he even experimented with LSD, using it as an entheogen to better understand God. If anyone could help me with this case it would be Twain. "The top and bottom incisor teeth were removed from the victims and used to form the numerals one through four—they were inlaid into each of the medallions."

"And you need to stop said villain before there is a number five, correct?"

"Once again, I'm not sure. The suspect is a man named Michael Tillerman. I've tied him to one of the murders. I also believe that he may be involved with the Jacoby slayings." I stood and beckoned for Twain to do the same. "Come with me, Nigel, I want to show you something."

"Where are we going?"

"Over to the crime lab."

He smiled. "Sightseeing—I love it."

Twain and I strolled down the corridor together. I walk briskly, but Twain had no trouble staying with me; his strides were long and purposeful. "So what's new in your life, Nigel? We always talk about me. I haven't been a very good friend."

"Nonsense, Stephanie, you've been a splendid friend."

I smiled at Twain. "Seeing anyone?" *Damn, girl, did you have to ask? Prying a bit?*

Twain searched my eyes as if to say, *are we playing that game again?* It seemed we were doomed to an eternal game of cat and mouse: testing, teasing, and probing our thoughts and desires. Too bad it couldn't go anywhere. "I date."

"Anyone in particular?"

"I'm seeing this young woman from Barbados, but it's just a fling."

"Why just a fling?" *Thank God it's nothing serious.*

"She's fifteen years my junior. The sex is phenomenal, but that's where it stops. She wants to be a recording artist . . . the next Rhianna, I think. We don't have all that much in common."

Jesus, did he have to say that? Now all I could think about was Twain tossing it up under the sheets with a gorgeous young thing who looks like Rhianna. *Shit, I'm so jealous. Maybe I can get her name, friend her on Facebook, and see if she'll tell me what sex with Nigel is like. If it's good and juicy, maybe we can coauthor a book and call it Fifty Shades of Twain.* "So you're just using her for the sex?"

Twain gave me a devilish smile. "Maybe she's the one using me. Anyway, my heart belongs to another. Alas, it can never be."

Twain never said that I was the one he longed for, but I took it that way. I turned away so that he didn't see that I was blushing. Thank God we had arrived at the lab.

I showed Twain the two six-sided vases. The lab had already processed them; the dried lilies had been removed, and the vases were clean. I pointed to the first vase. "This vase was found in the Jacoby home." I pointed to the second vase. "This one was found in Michael Tillerman's abandoned home."

Twain looked closely at both vases. "Can I touch them?"

"Yes, they've already been processed—help yourself."

Twain took a few moments to examine each vase, checking them from every conceivable angle.

"What do you think, Nigel?"

"They're lovely, lead crystal, I believe, and beautifully manufactured."

I gave him a playful elbow in the side. "C'mon, seriously."

"I can only state the obvious; they appear to be identical. The basic design is of a hexagram, which may have religious and spiritual connotations."

"Both vases contained the same small lilies."

Twain smiled. "Let me guess . . . the Seal of Solomon, Polygonatum multiflorum?"

Jesus, and they call me a witch. I nodded. "That's a pretty good goddamn guess."

"I was just following the religious connection. It's unlikely to be coincidental. Polygonatum multiflorum is rarely used by florists."

"Zugg said the same thing."

He shrugged. "The chance of two identical vases filled with the same uncommon variety of lily in both homes is so remote as to approach zero."

"We now have DNA evidence reports on all of the unidentified victims. The three male victims were Jewish. It's likely the female was Jewish too but we can't be certain. Somehow I need to find something in this that will help me to track down Tillerman."

Twain was quiet for a minute. "Tell me, Stephanie, how were these four victim's murdered?"

"We don't know how the first victim was murdered but the medallion with numeral one was made of mortar from the victim's bones."

Twain closed his eyes. I could see that he was straining to recall something. "By the sweat of your brow you will eat your food until you return to the ground, since from it you were taken; for dust you are and to dust you will return. Genesis 3:19. And the next?"

"The second body was found in Kowsky Plaza in lower Manhattan. The medallion was around the victim's neck. The victim died of hypothermia. He froze to death."

"Go on."

"The third was recovered from a funeral parlor. The victim had been burned alive in a cremation furnace."

"Ouch! And the last?" Twain's eyes were still closed.

"The last victim was a woman. She was found in the Staten Island Narrows. She was wearing scuba gear. Her lungs had exploded due to rapid ascent."

Twain opened his eyes. "I may have something."

"Tell me," I said excitedly. *"What?"*

"'The Seal of Solomon is not so much a star as it is a pair of inverted triangles. The Jewish Kabbalists called Solomon's Seal the Mystery of all Mysteries, a geometric synthesis of the entire occult doctrine."

Oh great, not the occult doctrine. The occult doctrine was the bible for every lunatic and serial crazy on the street. *Just what I needed to hear.* "Explain please."

"The mystery of all mysteries, Stephanie, the connection from life to death . . . and perhaps from death back to life."

As I listened to Twain the light bulb went off in my head. I thought about each of the four victims—we knew how three of them were murdered. "Victim number two was frozen, in effect killed by water. Victim number three was burnt, killed by fire. Victim number four was killed when her lungs exploded . . . air." Twain smiled at me with pride as I expanded upon his line of thinking. "We don't know how victim number one was killed, but his body was reduced to dust. As you kind of said, to the earth you shall return."

"That's right. According to lore, the interlaced

triangles represent the four earth elements," Twain said. "The top point of the triangle represents fire. The bottom represents water. The left represents air and the right represents earth."

"Tillerman made four sacrifices, one for each of the four earth elements. Do you think?"

"I do."

The idea was so bizarre, and yet in some demented way, it actually made sense—Michael Tillerman was trying to bring someone back to life.

Chapter Fifty-four

We followed the K-9 dogs twenty yards into the greenbelt until they found the spot. The digging began immediately. Gus and I waited while shovelful after shovelful of earth was removed from the ground. A biker had seen what he described as "a giant digging a hole." He had seen Tillerman's wanted poster on TV and called the Most Wanted hotline.

"Who do you think we'll find down there?" Gus asked.

"Honestly, I hope they dig up an old pair of boots. I am just so tired of finding bodies. I don't think I can take any more."

"Old boots? You mean as in old war boots?"

Actually the image of a pair of Christian Louboutin boots popped into my head, but I wasn't going to admit that to Gus. Besides, the ground was muddy, and I just couldn't contemplate soiling a gorgeous pair of fine leather boots like that. "Yes, like old war boots. Discarded boots that no one wants."

"That's not like you."

"I know, but my legs are cramping so I can't think about a pair of Joan Crawford F-me pumps right now."

"How about later?" Gus displayed an impish smile.

"Really? How can you think of sex at a time like this? Eight people are dead, maybe nine, and a maniac is running around killing people, hoping to bring someone back to life. That doesn't stymie your libido?"

"I can picture you in a pair of thigh-high boots and a

lacy, black teddy. Nothing can slow me down when it comes to the thought of ravaging your body. I honestly don't give a tinker's damn."

"A tinker's damn? Do you even know what a tinker is?"

"Does it matter?"

"No." I whispered in his ear. "Catch Tillerman, and I'll wear anything you like. Now pay attention and focus on the case."

"Thanks for the incentive." Gus smiled and pinched my butt. *Men! My God. There's a time and a place for everything, isn't there?*

"So who do you think Tillerman might be trying to reanimate?" Gus asked with a smirk. "I can't believe how fucking crazy this guy is."

"His family is unaccounted for; they'd be at the top of my list."

"Don't you think there would be a record of three murders?"

"You'd think." I shrugged. "You and I both know there are bodies buried everywhere. There are lots of victims the police don't know about. It wouldn't surprise me if this goofball kept their deaths a secret. The questions are: who killed them and how did they die?"

I saw Sonellio approaching from the corner of my eye. He wore a warm-up suit, but his appearance was anything but athletic. It looked as if his stamina was at a minimum. He walked lifelessly and carried a small oxygen tank. His complexion appeared ashen. I walked over and put my arm through his. "Hi, boss, out for a stroll?"

He smiled at me but did not reply because getting around was obviously such a struggle for him. We walked back to where Gus was standing. Gus rubbed Sonellio's shoulder, and we waited as the hole was excavated. Sonellio's posture frightened me. He looked so feeble, as if he might fall over at any second. I pulled him close to me and with that gesture said what I wouldn't dare say aloud. *I'm here for you, my old friend. Lean on me.*

Again he was silent, but his eyes said, *thank you.*

They stopped digging. My heart stumbled as a body was lifted out of the hole. It was the very last thing I expected to see: a medical examiner's black body bag. They unzipped it and there staring up at us were the lifeless eyes of Bruce Jacoby, husband, father and murder victim. My eyes widened. I turned to Gus to express my disbelief. Just then I felt a tug on my arm. Sonellio was going down. I grabbed him to soften the fall. Gus moved quickly and prevented him from hitting his head.

Gus began to work on him. "Boss, boss, stay with us . . . boss!" My eyes met Gus'—in that glance, we understood each other's concern. "Call an ambulance," Gus called out to the other policemen at the scene.

Time seemed to stand still. I felt the breath catch in my lungs, and my heart began to race. My throat tightened, and then when I least expected it, I felt the baby kick.

Chapter Fifty-five

I walked into the pub across the street from the hospital and sat down at the bar. The bartender greeted me with the ever popular, "What'll it be?"

"Bourbon neat and a dozen Quaaludes."

He was reaching for a bottle of Maker's Mark when it hit him, "What? Did you say . . .?" He angled his head. "I don't think I heard you right."

"The bourbon is for my boyfriend. He'll be here in a minute. I was just kidding about the 'ludes."

He glanced through the pub front window across the street to the hospital. "Bad day?" the bartender asked with a sympathetic smile. "Sorry to hear it. And for you?"

"Just sparkling water. The child developing in my womb gets bent out of shape when I imbibe."

He leaned over the bar and glanced at my belly. "Congratulations! Hey, I make a killer frozen piña colada—virgin, of course. Let me make one for you. It's on me."

"Piña colada, you say. I don't know—that's an awful lot of sugar."

"I'm telling you, it's amazing. I used to make them for my wife when she was pregnant."

"Okay, thanks." I was in dire need of a brain freeze, anything to numb my mind to the painful news we had just heard. Sonellio's cancer had spread. It was in his liver, blocking the portal vein. I didn't know if he would live long enough to see Tillerman brought to justice. Toni had called her daughters to let them know the end was near. Sonellio's girls were making plans to fly in from out of town.

Gus found me at the bar and sat down in front of his drink. "Are you going to be okay?"

I grabbed his arm and laid my head against it. "Jesus, Gus, I hurt all over. I want to go home and cry."

Gus stroked my hair. "I understand." He kissed my head. "Nothing is going to make this any easier."

I had been there before. I remembered feeling the same way when we found out my father had run out of time. Familiarity didn't make it any easier to deal with. I was dying on the inside all over again. The bartender put my tall and frosty piña colada on the bar. It looked so good that I could taste it before the straw was to my lips.

"The bartender smiled hopefully. "How is it?"

I could almost feel the capillaries in my brain freeze. "Amazing. It's just what I needed." Gus introduced himself. A good bartender knows when to chat and when to take a hike. He left us and moved down the bar so that we could have some sorely needed peace and quiet. We sat in silence for a while. Gus nursed his bourbon. I stared off into space. Nothing would make this day any better. We just had to slog through it.

"So why do you think Tillerman buried Mr. Jacoby? I mean why go through all the trouble of stealing a body only to discard it?"

"I don't know." The chemicals in my brain were out of balance. The thinking process had been temporarily suspended. "Nothing about this case makes sense to me at the moment, but keep talking, okay? I need the distraction."

"Sure," Gus said. "The ME's office said that the body did not appear to be tampered with."

"Even stranger, don't you think?"

Gus shrugged and signaled for a refill. My phone rang. I didn't recognize the caller's number and was tempted to let it go to voicemail. It rang three times . . . four, five, "Detective Chalice. How can I help you?"

"Detective Chalice, it's Cathy, the waitress from the diner. Do you remember me?"

My mind filled with the vision of an elderly man bent over a cup of soup. I actually imagined that I could hear him slurping. "Yes, Cathy, how can I help you?"

"I think that you're still looking for Michael Tillerman, aren't you?"

"Yes, we are. Why?"

"Well, I remembered something. I don't know if it's important but I figured it couldn't do any harm to let you know."

"You were right to call, Cathy. What did you remember?"

"Tillerman used to hang around with some disabled guy. I'm not sure about his name but I think his father owns that Italian gentlemen's club, Café Baci."

Baci? Why does that sound familiar? I remembered the delicious tiramisu and the name of the man I'd met at Sonellio's home, Giacomo Babocci. I didn't know that he had a disabled son. "How was this man disabled?" I asked.

"He has an artificial arm and leg. I'm not sure, but I think he's a war veteran. I used to see the two of them building stuff in Tillerman's garage. Does that help?"

"It definitely does. Thank you, Cathy. Is this your cell phone number? I want to make a note of your contact information."

"Yes."

I thanked her again and hung up.

"What was that?" Gus asked. He had a disconcerted look on his face, and I could see that the bourbon had hit him right between the eyes.

“Hand me the car keys, handsome.” “I’ll explain along the way.”

Chapter Fifty-six

Café Baci was located on a commercial street along with other neighborhood shops, centered between a shoe repair store and a dry cleaner. Each and every patron went silent when I walked through the door of the café. I had forgotten that the establishment was for men only, but none of that mattered. The sexist, old-world patrons would just have to deal with the fact that a pregnant law enforcement officer was desecrating their sacred gentlemen's club.

A waiter tried to keep me from entering the club, but I had my shield in his face and Gus Lido at my back. "I'm sorry," the waiter said. "This *ristorante* is for gentlemen only."

"I need to see Mr. Babocci immediately. Police business. Tell him Detective Chalice is here to see him."

The waiter seemed to panic. "Oh my God. Please wait right here. I'll get him." He turned and walked through the swinging kitchen door.

Babocci walked out within a minute. He pulled on his jacket as he crossed the restaurant floor. He gestured to the door. "Outside, detectives . . . please." These old Italians take their traditions very seriously. It wouldn't surprise me if Babocci had a priest come over to exorcise the place after I was gone. We followed him outside and away from the restaurant. We were standing in front of the dry cleaning store next door. "Is this about Nick?" he asked. "What's going on?"

"I'm afraid that Nick's taken a turn for the worse.

He's back in the hospital, but that's not why we're here."

"Then what?" he said impatiently. "Can't you see that I've got a business to run?"

I ran a check on Babocci's son on the ride over from the hospital and learned that his son Tommaso had been released from the army on a medical discharge. "We have reason to believe that your son Tommaso may have had a personal relationship with Michael Tillerman. We need to speak with him immediately."

Babocci's eyes filled with rage. "What? Are you kidding me? You think my son Tom knows this animal? That's fucking ridiculous. He was out with me trying to find Tillerman the other night. *Madonna*," he swore and bit his clenched fist in anger. "Why if you didn't know Nick, I'd—"

Gus stepped between us. "I'm Detective Lido and you'd what?" he yelled. "Where the fuck do you get off talking to a police officer like that?" Gus was just being protective—okay, overly protective—but you could understand his reason.

"Is he inside, Giacomo? I need to talk with him now."

Babocci was hot enough to explode. His chest was heaving, and his face was blood red. "No. He's not here." It took him a second before he offered more information. "Follow me. He's probably home." He walked back to the café and whispered to one of the waiters. He didn't look at us as he crossed the boulevard and got into his car.

Chapter Fifty-seven

Babocci drove his Cadillac as if it were stolen. We followed him as he flew down one street after another, through stop signs and red lights. I guess he figured the police escort gave him carte blanche to break every traffic law on the books—I was certain that he would wear out a set of tires by the time he arrived home.

"Thanks for having my back, Gus." I smiled at him. "I guess that you didn't like him roughing up the mother of your child."

Gus shook his head. "I understand the guy is old school, but he showed a total lack of respect. You didn't accuse his son of child molesting. I think it was pretty clear. We need to speak to his kid because he might have information that will help us to apprehend a coldblooded murderer."

"He's not the first guy to get a little rough with me. I'm a big girl, you know."

"Yeah, I know that you can handle yourself. It's just—"

I smiled knowingly. "I know. It's the baby. I'm going back behind a desk after this one's over—just until the baby is born. I don't like taking chances with the baby's life and I don't want to put you at additional risk because you're worried about me."

"Have you felt anymore kicking?"

I smiled and nodded. "Yup." I had no qualms about remaining on active duty up until then, but everything changed when I felt that first kick. Lieutenant Shearson would get her way after all. I had Ma and Ricky, the most loving support system in the world, ready and waiting in the wings. I love my job and am determined to stay on the force until life or love dictates that I can't do it anymore, but for the near-term I was going to maintain a low profile.

A text message from Ambler popped up on my cell phone. *News flash: we cross-referenced a list of the test trial meds stolen from Vicor with a list of patients on the same meds. You were right, Stephanie—Tillerman's name popped up. He's taking a powerful antidepressant called Repressor. We spoke with the psychiatrist who recommended him for the trial, and he said that Tillerman was severely depressed over the murder of his wife and two sons. He may be trying to bring his family back to life.*

Babocci's Cadillac screeched as it slowed down. It hit bottom as it bounced up the driveway. The door opened, and Babocci flew out. We were hot on his heels, behind him as he inserted the key into the door lock. I didn't even have a second to tell Gus about Ambler's message.

"Tommy, Tommy," he yelled into the darkened house. He flipped on the light switch. "Tommy, you home?" He entered with determined steps. "I don't think he's here." He turned and glared at us. "Do you have any idea what my kid has been through? He lost an arm and a leg defending his country, and my wife Angela died just before Christmas."

I felt for Babocci and his son. Unfortunately there was a mass murderer on the loose, and we needed to do what we needed to do. "I wish there was another way, Giacomo, but there isn't."

"Yeah, yeah," Babocci said as he continued to walk through the house. "Like you really give a shit . . . Yo, Tommy, you here?" He opened the basement door. The three of us stood at the top of the basement staircase, looking down. “The basement is dark. He’s not home.”

“Can you give him a call on his cell phone?” Gus asked. “This is important.”

“Sure, what the hell,” Babocci said. He wandered toward the kitchen as he pulled his cell phone from his pocket. Gus and I waited by the basement stairs. Perhaps my senses were heightened because of the pregnancy, but I was pretty sure that I smelled the distinctive odor of formaldehyde coming from the basement. It was faint but not so faint as to be missed by a pregnant bloodhound cop.

Babocci returned a moment later. “I got his voicemail. I left him a message.”

“There’s an odd odor coming from the basement,” I said. “Do you mind if we take a look down there?”

Babocci’s eyes grew wild again. “My house smells? Holy shit! Are you kidding or what?” He sniffed the air. “He paints. You want to investigate his work? Are you some kind of art detective? Give me a break, will ya?”

“I just want to have a look around. It doesn’t smell like paint to me. It smells like formaldehyde. Can we have a look?”

“Can you have a look? No! My son’s work is very private. I’m the only one he lets down there. Painting is the only thing that makes him happy. You know what he’s got down there? He’s got paint and canvas, that’s what he’s got down there. There’s a carton of catheters down there too, because some Arab motherfucker shot off his penis and testicles after he rescued a family of Israelis. You want to see that too?”

I thought Babocci would have a stroke. “Please, Giacomo, try to settle down. I’m not trying to insult you.” The word Israelis resounded with me. All of Tillerman’s victim’s were likely Jewish. I wasn’t sure if there was a connection but the possibility of one made me push harder. “Please, Giacomo, it’s easier this way. Two minutes, and we’re in and out. You’re Nick’s friend. The last thing I want to do is call a judge for a search warrant.”

“Go!” he said with a furious hand gesture. “Don’t you dare touch his paintings. Nothing, understand?”

“We’ll respect his work,” Gus said.

I flipped on the lights and started down the stairs. Gus and Babocci followed me.

The basement was a large, cavernous room. Tom Babocci was a prolific painter. Completed canvases were hung on the basement walls and several were leaning against the base of the wall. The focal point of his work was a large glass painting of a weathered house standing at the water’s edge. “Your son is very talented, Giacomo. His work is beautiful.” Tom’s work was truly compelling. As I looked at the different canvases, I noticed that he painted in a variety of styles. I saw abstract human forms and landscapes—he seemed to have a very active imagination.

The odor of formaldehyde grew stronger as I approached the large glass painting. “Don’t go near that,” Babocci warned. “It’s glass.”

I’m pregnant, not clumsy! The glass panel was set into a metal frame, which was affixed to support columns on either side. “It looks pretty sturdy to me.” I could see that Babocci was unhappy, but it didn’t keep me from taking a closer look. The colors in the painting were rich shades of blue and white that drew my interest. As I got closer, I could see that the paint had not been applied with brush strokes but rather by the application of small dots. The windows in the painted house looked incredibly natural. The window frames were dark blue. The windows themselves had a sparse application of blue pinpoints. The area behind the painting was pitch black. The glass itself was transparent, and it made the painted windows look like the windows of an actual darkened house.

"You're too close," Babocci called out, but I was completely drawn to the painting, by its colors and technique. I could not back away. As I stared at the windows, a thought popped into my head. I illuminated my searchlight and peered through one of the windows in the painting, as I would if I were looking through the window of a real house. I put my eye up to the glass and looked through it. The body of a massive man had been positioned on a sofa—There was only one person it could be. He was wearing a white cloak. Michael Tillerman's angry, tormented mind had finally found peace . . . and he was seated with his family.

Chapter Fifty-eight

Thunder boomed so loudly that the windows in my apartment rattled. It awoke me, and in those scant seconds between slumber and consciousness all the events of the past few hours flooded back into my mind. It was as if I were still in Babocci's basement, holding my searchlight on the large painting, and peering through the window of the house that had been painted upon it. The body of Michael Tillerman had been positioned on the end of a sofa. Sitting next to him were the bodies of his wife Barbara and his two children Mark and Stephen. They had all been mummified.

The moments that followed the discovery were still excruciatingly vivid. Giacomo Babocci had insisted that he stay to watch the NYPD tactical team unbolt the large glass panel from where it had been affixed to the support columns of the foundation. He had been forced to endure the gruesome reality that a family had been murdered and deposited in the basement of his house. How long had the bodies been there? Who killed Tillerman's wife and children? Who had killed Tillerman? At the moment, all fingers were pointed to Tom Babocci, the war hero who had rescued an Israeli family and lost his arm, leg, and manhood in the process. Was it any wonder he had lost his mind? The army had taken more than his limbs—it had taken his sanity. It had taken his life and any hope of having a normal future.

I could see Giacomo Babocci's tortured and miserable face as if he were standing in front of me. I could see the tears running down his cheeks. I could see his red eyes and the painful reality he was unable to accept—his son was a murderer. His son was twisted. “How could I not know?” he said. “Tommy,” he cried. “How could you?” He listened to me make the phone calls to the FBI and police department. He listened when I gave the instructions to switch the manhunt from Michael Tillerman to his son. Babocci tried to reach his son on the phone but was unsuccessful with several attempts. Wherever Tom Babocci was, he did not want to be found.

It was about four in the morning. I had been asleep about ninety-minutes, about one complete cycle. I toyed with the idea of going back to sleep but knew better. My mind was racing, and my heart was beating quickly. I looked down at Gus. He was sound asleep. The phone rang. I grabbed my cell phone and sprang from the bed. I answered and pulled the bedroom door closed behind me so that I wouldn’t wake him. I recognized the name on the display. It was Toni Sonellio. The boss was either gone or just moments away from the end. “Hi, Toni,” I said apprehensively.

She said just two words, “Come now.”

It took a moment until the knot in my throat relaxed enough for me to speak. “We’ll be right there.” I sighed and walked back into the bedroom to wake Gus.

Chapter Fifty-nine

Toni was asleep in the chair next to her husband's bed when Gus and I arrived at the hospital. The boss was perfectly still in his hospital bed. The sound of his wheezing and the beat of the heart monitor told me that he was still alive. We tiptoed into the room. I knew that Toni was exhausted and wanted desperately not to disturb her, but she sensed our presence and woke up. We were in each other's arms, crying and trying to share a little strength with each other. I could only remember hurting this badly when my father died. Toni looked at her husband. "I'm sure he knows that you're here."

"I know."

"My daughters are on the way. I hope—" Her voice trailed off, smothered by emotion.

"It will be all right," Gus said. He looked past her to me. His expression showed that he felt helpless. We were all helpless. Only God knew if he would hold on long enough to say goodbye to his children.

"Gus, why don't you take Toni downstairs for some coffee. I'll wait here."

"I'm okay," Toni said, but I could see that she was emotionally exhausted and needed to take a break.

I put my hand on her arm. "If I know the boss, he'll tough it out until his daughters get here. I'll call if you need to hurry back."

"Are you sure?" Toni asked.

I nodded.

Gus put his arm around her waist. "Come on, Toni,

Stephanie's kicking us out." He smiled at me sadly as he directed her out the door. He knew that there was more to my request than just giving Toni a short break—I needed a few minutes to say goodbye.

As I looked out the hospital window at the sobering morning sky, I wondered why God would allow this to happen. I was losing all of the great men in my life, one by one: first my dad and now Sonellio. He had always meant so much to me. He was like the uncle I never had, one of my father's contemporaries, and a guiding force in my life.

I swallowed, hoping the pop in my ears would block out the monotonous beep of the heart monitor. It was early in the morning, so damn early, not quite six. *Too early to lose him*, I told myself. *Please give us the day, just one more day. I'm not ready.* I turned from the window to drink him in, perhaps for the last time, and hope for a miracle. His face was pale. Each breath was so tentative that I was uncertain another would follow.

I folded my arms over my belly as if to protect the new life within from the influence of death. "He's a good man," I whispered, "a really good man." A few tears began to drizzle down my cheek.

The baby kicked.

"Don't be upset, there's nothing we can do."

The baby kicked again as if to challenge me.

"Settle down." I rubbed my belly in a soothing manner. "You're just like your father, always looking for attention."

God takes with one hand and gives back with the other, one life ebbing away and a new one about to arrive. Anyone in my position would have entertained the same thought.

"What's that you say, I'm being morose? You know you're very precocious for a fetus."

The baby kicked twice in rapid succession.

"Anyway, I'm sorry if I'm sad. I can't help it. I love him a lot."

I heard the floor creak. I was still a little on edge from the events that had just transpired. To say there were loose ends in our investigation was an understatement. A murderer was still at large. I usually have my emotions under control, but with all of my hormones whirling around like spirits in a cocktail shaker . . . I turned and looked through the doorway into the hospital corridor. All was quiet.

Sonellio moaned. His desperate sound drew my attention. I stroked his cheek. "Nothing to worry about, boss, everything will be all right."

Thinking back, Sonellio had always been around. My father had worked for him when he was on the job. He had always been there for me after dad passed.

"Hey, stop kicking," I scolded the baby playfully. "I'm going to miss him. I'm sorry." He became my boss after I made the cut and became a detective. He was a good, salt-of-the-earth, church-going, Italian boy with great morals. But Sonellio had smoked heavily. It was a solitary chink in the armor of a noble man, a weakness that was going to put him into the ground. Lung cancer. It could have all been prevented. It was difficult to remember him as the healthy, younger man I had once known. *To see him now, so gaunt; you would never believe it was the same person.*

"You're never going to smoke," I informed the baby.

I felt the baby move.

"It's not negotiable."

My stomach rumbled. This time it was due to hunger. "I hope daddy gets here with mommy's coffee soon. It's okay, Sweetie; it's only decaf. Yes, that's right. I've given up regular coffee, just for you."

The baby was still trying to get comfortable.

"Anything for you, Sweetie."

The baby grew fidgety.

"Yes, even the red wine; that's gone too. No, I don't mind."

Sonellio moaned again, more deeply than before, and I wondered if he was out of time. He had been moaning since I arrived, a low and even sound that accompanied his shallow breathing. He moaned again, louder still. There was something unnerving about the sound of it. It sounded as if he was agitated. It was almost as if he sensed something and was trying to give me a warning.

The baby abruptly stopped fidgeting and became calm.

I felt goose bumps rise on my arms and neck.

"Chalice!"

My heart skipped a beat. I was waiting for Gus to return and was expecting to hear the loving tone of his voice.

The voice I heard was not his.

There was something disturbing and strange in the sound of the voice I had just heard. My heart became still.

It seemed like seconds passed.

My heart finally began to beat again.

I turned.

My eyes locked on the gun that was pointed at my baby and me. I instinctively covered my belly with my hands to protect my baby as any mother would, but we were out in the open, naked and vulnerable. I cried out in terror, *"Gus!"*

And then I heard the sound of the gun fire.

I hit the floor and heard the sound of shattering glass. The bullet missed us and gone through the window. I heard footsteps racing down the corridor.

"Stephanie!" I heard Gus calling out to me, a desperate cry for my safety and for the safety of our child. I could see under the hospital bed. My assailant was gone. Gus came charging through the doorway. He helped me off the floor. "My God, are you all right?" He stared at me with an incredulous expression, waiting desperately for me to put him at ease. Wind rushed through the shattered window.

"I'm okay."

He still looked worried. "And the baby?"

"I braced for the fall with my hands. We're both okay."

"You're sure?"

"Yes, I'm sure."

"Did you see who it was?"

"No, the shooter wore a ski mask."

"Shit."

"But he called out to me before he fired. I think I know who it is."

Chapter Sixty

"**It** sounded like Babocci, but I'm not sure. His voice was muffled by the mask."

"Could it have been his son?"

"Maybe. I don't know. I never met his son. Babocci's café is just blocks from here."

We made a quick call for assistance. The hospital staff was on top of the situation—they rolled the boss into another room within minutes. Toni was hysterical. I can't tell you why I wasn't equally unnerved. I suppose it was the call to action that distracted me from my emotions. Something deep down inside was pulling at me, desperately trying to point me in the right direction. "Can you stay with them until backup arrives?"

"You're incredible," Gus said. "Do you actually think I'd let you go alone? There's no way in hell."

I saw the look of admonishment on his face. "All right, I'll get the car out of the parking lot and wait for you by the front entrance. Backup should be here any minute."

"Fine," Gus said. "I'll meet you at the car."

I hit the staircase and raced down the stairs to the main level. The stamina I had built up from years of exercise and running was still with me. I broke into a sprint and raced to our car. I pulled around to the front of the building and alerted Ambler and Forzo to the new developments. Gus was getting into the car by the time I completed the second call.

"I just got off the phone with Forzo. He's sending

every available unit to Babocci's restaurant. We're very close. We'll probably get there before any of Forzo's units respond." The engine was running—I threw the car into gear and floored the accelerator. The car smacked down hard as I zoomed through the intersection and sped off toward Café Baci. Forzo's people would have Babocci's license plate number from DMV within minutes. Forzo would have every unit under his command on the street and looking for Babocci's car. Time was of the essence. I wasn't sure if we would find him at the café, but my gut told me we would.

I had the lights and siren on as we raced toward Café Baci. I had been there hours earlier and was able to navigate the route as if I were on autopilot. I slammed on the brakes as we pulled up in front of the café. The lights were off and the door was locked but we were in pursuit of a felon. Gus broke the glass door with the back end of his Maglite, reached in, and unlocked it. "Stay behind me," he said. "Got it?"

"Got it." We entered the café and used our searchlight beacons to look around. It was almost dawn, but the heavy draperies on the front windows kept the interior dark. We proceeded through the seating area and cautiously made our way into the kitchen. There were no windows in the kitchen—it was completely dark. I found the light switch, but it was smashed and inoperative. I pulled open the door of the huge walk-in refrigerator. Gus looked inside while I covered him.

"Clear," he said.

He was still in the refrigerator when shots rang out in the dark. I stumbled as I backed behind the counter to take cover and accidentally pushed the refrigerator door shut with Gus inside. I heard Gus scream just as the door closed. I couldn't tell what his scream meant. Was he calling out for me or was he . . . *Oh dear God, no!*

I was pinned down while the shooter sprayed the area with bullets. "Gus?" I called out in panic. "Gus, talk to me." *He can't hear me in there*, I thought . . . *I hope that's all it is*. I didn't want to allow the thought to enter my head but it forced its way in. *He's been shot. He might be dead.* I felt my body go limp. A round zinged by, not far from my foot, and brought me back into the moment. I couldn't see the shooter, but I could tell the direction the shots were coming from. He had me pinned behind the preparation counter. He had fired several rounds, but I didn't know how many he had left. I couldn't stand up—it would have given him a clear shot at me. I fired blindly over the top of the counter, hoping that God would aim for me. I heard a shriek, followed by the creaking of rusted hinges. Light flooded into the kitchen. I could hear the shooter running down steps.

I crawled over to the refrigerator and opened the door. Gus was lying on the floor. He was clutching his right arm and his automatic was lying on the floor next to him. He must have seen the panic on my face. "I'm okay," he said preemptively. "The bullet hit me in the arm."

I knelt next to him while I kept my gun aimed at the refrigerator opening. I tore away his sleeve and examined his arm. "Okay? You're bleeding like a pig." The bleeding was bad, but not terrible. "Thank God—I think it missed the brachial artery." The brachial artery is the major blood vessel in the upper arm. Had the bullet torn it . . . I didn't want to think of the possibility. I picked up his gun and put it in his left hand. "I hope you're ambidextrous."

Gus pointed the gun at the refrigerator opening. "Not a problem."

"We need to stop the bleeding." I spotted a clean dishrag and a spool of cooking string. I wrapped the dishrag around his arm and tied it tight with the cooking string. “That will have to do.” The bleeding slowed significantly. I stood. “You can’t stay in here.” Let’s get you up on your feet.” His blood pressure must have been very low because he wobbled and almost went down when he tried to stand. I helped him maneuver over to a vegetable crate and sat him down on it with his back against the refrigerator wall. “I guess you’ll be okay in here for a few minutes with the door open. I’ll be right back.”

“Stephanie, where are you going? Backup will be here any minute.” He looked into my eyes, and then he went out. I checked his pulse. It was slow and even.

“I’ve got this one, Gus,” I said. “I’m going to take care of business.”

Light from the basement staircase now illuminated the kitchen. The shooter must have been hiding on the other side of the basement door when we entered the kitchen, and then he opened fire when he thought he had us pinned down. I was cautiously making my way down the stairs when I heard the sound of a light bulb being smashed, and once again everything went black. I felt my heart knock within my chest, and it took seconds until I was courageous enough to move forward. I clicked on my Maglite and proceeded down the stairs. I held the Maglite level with my gun, but the corona of the beam illuminated the wooden steps at my feet. *I hit him.* There were drops of blood on the stairs.

There were shadows at the far end of the room. In the distance between the shadows, I saw the man in the ski mask standing in front of a large, sliding steel door. *A door to where?* He stood with his back to me. My ears were just sensitive enough to hear that he was fumbling with a key, trying to insert it into a lock. “Stop! This place will be swarming with cops in a minute. Don’t make this worse than it already is."

He looked back at me for a second, and then he was gone. He had slid the door open and closed it within seconds. I crossed the basement to pursue him. A shot rang out on the other side of the door just as I reached for the door handle. *Oh, Jesus, what now?* I braced myself for a shock. *Stay low. Use the door for cover.* I slowly pulled back the door while I stood behind it and used it to shield my body. The first thing I saw was the shooter's eyes behind the mask staring through the darkness. When I hit him with my searchlight beam, the gun tumbled from his hand. He clutched his gut. Blood poured through his fingers.

The room was filled with metal tables and tanks of chemicals. The stench of petrochemical pervaded the air. A large glass painting stood behind him. It looked identical to the one Tom Babocci had painted as a final resting place for Michael Tillerman and his family.

"Why?" I asked.

The shooter's lips trembled when he spoke. "You couldn't understand." I was sure of the shooter's identity. It was Giacomo Babocci—I could tell from his voice. He pulled off the ski mask. I could see his stricken expression, and the abject sadness in his eyes. He teetered and then his weight shifted. He stumbled backward out of control. His inertia carried him into the large glass painting with such force that it shattered. He collapsed on the floor amidst a thousand bits of colored glass. I covered my mouth in horror. A couch had been hidden behind this painting just as with the one we had found earlier. Four embalmed bodies were positioned on the sofa: Sherri Jacoby, her two sons, and a man with an artificial arm.

I rushed over to Giacomo Babocci just as his gaze began to drift. "I did it for my boy," he said, and then his eyes froze. He was gone.

Chapter Sixty-one

I sat together with my family at the funeral of Chief of Detectives Nicholas Sonellio, the man I had and would always refer to as The Boss. He was a great man, a man whose impact I would feel forever. He was a man I would love unconditionally for as long as I lived.

Ma and Gus squeezed my hands as the priest eulogized my dear friend. The priest was a personal friend of the family and spoke of Nick with tenderness and reverence. In truth, I was not surprised when he concluded the eulogy the way he did.

"I visited Nick just a few days ago. He knew the end was near but refused to speak of it. He poured me coffee and anisette, and we sat and watched television together. As we watched one of his old favorites, I knew that I would speak these words when the time came . . . Nick Sonellio was a hero to all of us, but he had heroes of his own." He looked at Toni and her daughters with a fond smile. "These are the words of James T. Kirk, 'We are gathered here today to pay final respects to our honored dead. And yet it should be noted, in the midst of our sorrow, this death takes place in the shadow of new life, the sunrise of a new world; a world that our beloved comrade gave his life to protect and nourish.'"

Epilogue

The Memorial Day weekend promised to be glorious. Gus and I took a few days PTO, paid time off, the modern day term for vacation. *What's wrong with calling a vacation a vacation? Why does everything have to be reduced to an acronym? Vacation, holiday, trip, retreat, escape; I find all of those terms acceptable, but PTO? Puh-lease, give me a break.*

Several days had passed since I said goodbye to my dear friend Nick Sonellio. As you might imagine, I was having a hard time flipping the happy switch. I wanted to be happy. I yearned to be happy, but happiness seemed to elude me. Okay, I wasn't depressed, but I was melancholy and melancholy sucked, especially when you had everything in the world to be happy about and you just couldn't find your smile.

Gus packed for us and wouldn't tell me where we were headed, but I wasn't wearing a blindfold and we were on the Long Island Expressway headed east, so . . . "Where are we going?" I asked.

"It's a surprise."

"Of course, it's a surprise—that's just the point; I'm trying to guess."

"No guessing."

"No guessing? *What?* How about a hint?"

"No hints."

"Montauk?"

"No."

"The Hamptons?"

"No."

"No?"

"No!"

"Ooo, I've got it—the North Fork, wine country."

Gus snickered. "Nope. Why would I take you to the wine country if you can't drink?"

"I don't know, why would you tease me with a guessing game when you know that I hate it?"

"It doesn't seem as if you hate it."

"Well, I do."

"I think you're enjoying it."

"I'm not," I said with a silly smile on my face.

"You'll know soon enough."

"Fine. I just want you to know that there'll be no sex tonight."

Gus snorted. "Yeah, good one."

We got off the LIE and headed south on the Sagtikos Parkway. We were at least an hour from the East End of Long Island, so Montauk, the Hamptons, and the wine country were off the table. "I've got no clue."

"Fire Island."

I smacked his arm. "What? You told me just like that?"

"We'll be there in ten minutes—it'll be hard to keep it a secret when you see the ferry boat."

"Thanks, that sounds really nice." We had been there before and had a great time. I just hadn't remembered the directions. I gave him a peck on the cheek. "BTW, sex is back on my agenda."

"Big surprise." Gus rolled his eyes. "I don't know; I'll think about it."

I snickered.

We sat on the upper deck while the ferry made the trip from Bayshore to Fire Island. The sun was intense, but the breeze was sublime. I put on my Ray-Ban's and allowed the ocean breeze to intoxicate me. I began to feel happier and more at ease.

So much had happened since the conclusion of our investigation that I had not had time to fit all of the pieces together. With this case, as with many others, I could only hypothesize about the case elements, which could not be supported by physical evidence. I understood the motivation for Babocci's crimes the instant I dropped to the floor in Sonellio's hospital room. I used my hands to break my fall so as to protect my baby. As Babocci had said, "I did it for my boy." All he wanted was happiness for his son and to protect him from any more pain the world might inflict upon him—Tom Babocci had already suffered so much. For the criminally insane, the definition of happiness takes on an entirely different meaning. In his mind, his son Tom would never have the opportunity to live a happy life as the head of a family. So his father provided one for him.

The ballistics test run on the slugs recovered from the bodies of the Jacoby family matched Babocci's gun, but they did not match the slugs taken from the bodies of Michael Tillerman's family. Babocci may not have killed the Tillermans, or he may have used another weapon. Either way, he was able to convince a severely depressed Michael Tillerman not to report the murders to the police and managed to make him believe that he could help him bring his family back to life. Somewhere between grief, depression, and an overwhelming amount of mind-altering medication, Michael Tillerman snapped. He allowed himself to believe that if he killed four Jewish people he could bring his wife and children back to life. He did exactly that—he killed one for each of the four earth elements: earth, air, fire, and water. In reality, he was nothing more than a hapless accomplice in Babocci's plan—Tom Babocci had paid a heavy price for coming to the rescue of an Israeli family. I could only speculate that Babocci was following ancient law: an eye for an eye, a tooth for a tooth—four dead Jews to take the place of the family his son had liberated back in Iraq. Had Tom not saved them, he would have been on the first transport truck and would not have fallen prey to the Iraqi sniper. Tom Babocci's future would have been completely different.

The basement room in which Babocci had committed suicide was located under the adjacent dry cleaning store. Babocci owned both stores and leased the upstairs area to the dry cleaner. He retained the basement and used it for, shall we say, his more creative endeavors. Among the many items recovered and analyzed by the crime scene team were large saturation tanks, pressurized vats, compressors, and vacuum equipment, which Babocci used to plastinate his son, the Tillermans, and three members of the Jacoby family. Plastination is a mummification technique in which body tissues are saturated with silicone. It prevents the body tissue from decaying. The technique is widely used to prepare specimens for teaching hospitals and medical schools. Although we could not find evidence that Babocci received formal training in plastination, he was quite an accomplished artisan and would have had little trouble teaching himself the technique. The chemicals used in the process have a terrible odor. I suppose that the perchloroethylene used in the dry cleaning process masked the smell of chemicals in the basement.

My guess was that Tillerman embalmed the bodies of his family before turning them over to Babocci. It was a horrific assignment. Babocci must have convinced him that it was necessary. Tillerman's love for his family had to have been great in order for him to endure so much torment.

We also recovered the mold that had been used to fashion the four tablet-shaped pendants, which had been sent to the FBI. Here again I could only guess that at one time Babocci considered the possibility of setting up Tillerman for the four murders. Tillerman's capture would have put an end to the police investigation. It certainly would have prevented Babocci from becoming a suspect. I could only surmise that his compassion for Tillerman ultimately prevailed, and he made good on his promise to reunite Tillerman with his family, if only in a manner that Babocci considered acceptable. Babocci never counted on Tillerman's body being found—he and his family were to remain locked behind the painting forever. Tillerman had committed four murders and disposed of Bruce Jacoby's body so that Babocci's son Tom could replace him as the patriarch of a newly established family.

We found quantities of DMT, a fast-acting hallucinogenic drug and strychnine poison in that basement room as well as four urns marked with the Seal of Solomon. The plastination process made it impossible for the ME to check Tillerman's body for the presence of the two aforementioned chemical substances, but I'm convinced that Tillerman was drugged and poisoned—*I mean come on, how else do you take down an hombre of that size?* I prayed that Michael Tillerman found his family before he died, if only by way of a chemically induced hallucination. Giacomo Babocci lost his wife during the previous Christmas season. Perhaps her death was the trigger that sent him over the edge. We would never know for certain.

The ferry slowed as we approached the dock at Ocean Bay Park. I wanted to feel that ocean breeze forever. I was happy that I had begun to feel more like myself. Gus began to pick up our gear. "How's your arm?" I asked.

"Hurts like a mother," he said. "I could go for one of those rocket fuel cocktails over at Flynn's. You game?"

"Game on!" I said. I grabbed a backpack so that he wouldn't have to lift anything with his injured arm. I glared at him. "Don't even think about it."

Flynn's was just a short walk from the ferry. It was a popular place located right on the dock with an incredible view of the water.

The waitress was a pretty blonde, who wore an unbuttoned man-tailored shirt over a tiny bikini. She smiled at Gus as he approached. "Do you have a reservation?" she asked.

"Lido party," Gus said quietly.

Lido party?

She checked her list and then looked up. "Everyone's here." She turned and pointed to a large table in the corner of the outdoor deck.

I turned and saw six smiling faces: Ma, Ricky, Ambler, and a very scantily clad Marjorie Banks, Damien Zugg, and yes, the brutishly handsome Nigel Twain. They waved to us and toasted us with their cocktails. I got choked up and started to cry. I looked into Gus' eyes. "You did this for me?"

He had tears in his eyes as well. "I don't want you to be sad anymore."

I threw my arms around him. "How can I stay sad when I have you?" I kissed him on the lips. "I love you so much."

Ricky rushed over and handed us two frothy cold cocktails. "Yours is a virgin," he said, "for the baby."

I wiped the tears from my eyes and gave Ricky a kiss. "Thank you." I put my arm around him, and the three of us walked over to the table.

Ma was on her feet before we were halfway across

the floor. She grabbed me and planted a giant wet one on me. We went around the table, saying hello to all our friends. "I can't believe this," I said.

"Bah," Ma said in her feisty way. "And *I* can't believe how long it took you to get here. This is my third drink—I'm sloshed. What took you so long?"

I looked at Gus, and we both slammed our left hands down on the table. Ma's eyes bulged when she saw our gold bands. I glared at her, smiling and crying at the same time. "I told my husband not to speed."

About the Author

A resident New Yorker, Kelter often uses Manhattan and Long Island as backdrops for his stories. He has written four novels featuring street savvy NYPD Detective Stephanie Chalice: DON'T CLOSE YOUR EYES, RANSOM BEACH, THE BRAIN VAULT, and OUR HONORED DEAD.

BookWire Review wrote of the character, Stephanie Chalice, "Chalice's acerbic repartee is like an arsenal of nuclear missiles."

Early in his writing career, he received support from bestselling novelist, Nelson DeMille, who reviewed his work and actually put pencil to paper to assist in the editing of the first novel. DeMille said, "Lawrence Kelter is an exciting new novelist, who reminds me of an early Robert Ludlum."

His novels are quickly paced and feature a twist ending.

For more information, please visit the author at:
www.lawrencekelter.com or contact him by email at:
larrykelter@aol.com.

Made in the USA
Charleston, SC
24 December 2012